Mornay felt her cheeks begin to flame

Then his caressing hands were suddenly still. "I didn't mean this to happen, Mornay, believe me," Brad said.

"I—" she murmured, her voice choking. She realized that what had just happened was as entirely spontaneous for him as for her, and she fought desperately to rise above the most earth-shattering emotional experience of her life. Never had she been stirred to want a man before.

"Perhaps . . ." Amazingly, she found a light note somewhere. "Perhaps you'd better go."

She thought she saw a look in his eyes that admired the unconcerned way she was trying to treat the matter, but abruptly he stood up.

"Perhaps you're right."

Jessica Steele first tried her hand at writing romance novels at her husband's encouragement two years after they were married. She fondly remembers the day her first novel was accepted for publication. ''Peter mopped me up, and neither of us cooked that night,'' she recalls. ''We went out to dinner.'' She and her husband live in a hundred-year-old cottage in Worcestershire, and they've traveled to many fascinating places—such as China, Japan, Mexico and Denmark—that make wonderful settings for her books.

Books by Jessica Steele

HIDDEN HEART

Jessica Steele

Harlequin Books

TORONTO • NEW YORK • LONDON
AMSTERDAM • PARIS • SYDNEY • HAMBURG
STOCKHOLM • ATHENS • TOKYO • MILAN

Original hardcover edition published in 1990
by Mills & Boon Limited

ISBN 0-373-03114-9

Harlequin Romance first edition March 1991

HIDDEN HEART

CHAPTER ONE

MORNAY HAYNES awakened on that June morning, saw from the bedroom window in her small flat that the sky was blue, and sighed contentedly. She closed her eyes and snuggled down, intending to snatch another five minutes before she prepared to meet the challenge of another week.

Annoyingly, though, sleep eluded her. It was that word 'challenge' which struck a jarring note, she rather supposed. When she thought about it—and it didn't take much thinking about—she was forced to acknowledge that there was little that was challenging in her existence.

Mornay sat up in bed and contemplated the bed-covers. She was twenty-two, and had a nice, safe sec-retarial job working for nice, safe Mr Probert in the nice, safe surveyor's office at the town hall. She lived in a small flat in a nice part of the town of Reefingham—a flat found and approved of by her parents two years previously—and she had a nice, safe boyfriend—'dull' Claudia called him.

Torn between wanting to smile at pleasant thoughts of her sister Claudia, and feeling that she ought to frown at her sister's unflattering comments about nice and safe Robert Naylor, Mornay pushed the button down on her alarm clock before it could ring, and got out of bed.

Five minutes earlier, she mused, as she pattered to her bathroom, she had been quite content with her lot. Now, she felt decidedly dissatisfied.

Over her ablutions Mornay gave herself something of a lecture on how she should thank heavens for her present lot. Up until two years ago she had lived at home with her parents, who had the strictest views on how their two daughters should be brought up. Was it any wonder that Claudia had rebelled?

Mornay climbed out of the shower and dried her slender body, with her thoughts gentle on her sister. Claudia was five years older than herself and had been seventeen when, having come in late from a date, she'd had that last terrible row with her parents, and had left home.

'It's like living in a strait-jacket living in this house!' she had declared angrily to an unhappy twelve-year-old Mornay, who'd watched her adored elder sister throwing a few of her belongings into a suitcase.

'Where are you going?' Mornay had asked unhappily.

'I won't tell you that, love, because they'll only get it out of you,' Claudia had replied, 'and I don't want them turning up to tell me how ungrateful I am after all they've done for me. But—I won't forget you.'

She hadn't either, Mornay reflected as she munched on her usual piece of breakfast toast. Claudia was forever mentioned in the house, though not in a loving way but as an example of what she would become if she did not take heed of what her parents were telling her.

For a few months Mornay had experienced the confusion of having it drummed into her that Claudia was bad while at the same time only being able to remember the nice things that her big sister had done.

Then, two months after Claudia had left, Mornay had come out of school to see her sister waiting for her at the school gates and her confusion had disappeared like magic. As happiness entered her heart at seeing Claudia, she had no longer fretted whether she should hate or love her sister.

'Claudia!' she'd cried joyously.

'Does Mother still have her hair done on Friday?' Claudia had asked, giving her a hug.

Mornay had nodded. 'I'm supposed to go and have a cup of tea and a scone at the Blue Bird Café and meet her in an hour,' she'd replied. She would by far have preferred to go home and wait for her mother there, but she was not allowed to.

'Good,' Claudia had smiled. 'I could do with a cup of tea myself.'

There had followed many months of Mornay now looking forward to her Friday afternoon cup of tea with a scone. For now, with Claudia working at a job which gave her Friday afternoons off, Mornay always had her sister's company.

Claudia was still held up as a model not to be copied, however, and though on one never to be forgotten occasion Mornay tried to stick up for her, the lecture she subsequently received was long and exhausting. At the end of that sternest of lectures, Mornay was left in no doubt that her parents considered Claudia wayward, and was in no doubt that they were going to take the gravest care that she did not go the same way.

'Have you told the folks that you see me every Friday?' Claudia asked some months later, seeming to Mornay to be positively glowing, she looked so happy. Quickly, though, Claudia was cancelling out the fact that she had asked anything of the sort. 'That was a dumb question,' she grinned. 'Of course you haven't, or you wouldn't be here now.'

'Do you want me to tell them?' Mornay asked, happy in her sister's company and feeling then that she could do anything she asked of her. But Claudia shook her head.

'No,' she said, and was grinning again when she asked, 'Will they be home tonight if I drop round?'

'You're coming back?' Mornay asked, wide-eyed.

'Not on your life!' Claudia promptly knocked that lovely idea squarely on the head. 'I'm getting married, and since...'

'You're getting married!' Mornay squealed, excited and a week off her thirteenth birthday.

'Let everybody know!' Claudia laughed as a few genteel heads turned to look at them.

'But... Oh...' Mornay thought she had the answer. 'You're coming to ask the parents' permission.'

'I don't need it, I shall be eighteen the week after your birthday.'

Claudia then went on to tell her how Mr and Mrs Overton, Gerry's parents, although in no way as repressive in their attitude to their offspring as her own parents, liked 'things' done properly, and were insisting that the wedding was no hole-and-corner affair.

'Were it not for the fact that Gerry's parents have very generously said they'll give us the deposit for the most wonderful old house we want to buy over at Penny Dale, I'd get married without letting Mother and Father know,' Claudia revealed. 'But, as they do like things "nicely done", and since Gerry *is* their only chick, he and I will call round tonight to give my parents the good tidings.'

Five months after Claudia and Gerald Overton were married, Claudia gave birth to baby Emily. Mornay was delighted; Gerry's parents, after coming to terms with the situation, were delighted. Claudia and Gerry were supremely happy. The only people who were not overjoyed were Mornay's parents.

Nor were they overjoyed when, in direct contrast to her own overstrict upbringing, Claudia's daughter went through the first two years of her life without ever hearing the word 'discipline'. Emily was two years old when baby Alice was born, and once again everyone save Claudia's parents were delighted.

'It's to be hoped that they bring this one up better than that dreadful Emily,' Mrs Haynes sniffed, taking no pleasure in being a grandparent to a child she considered to be a little hooligan and not at all mollified that the blonde, curly-haired child looked the picture of health and happiness. Two years later, baby Florence arrived, and when another two years had gone by baby Prudence made her arrival on the scene.

'Mother still carping on?' Claudia had asked of the nineteen-year-old Mornay who had taken the bus the five miles to Penny Dale to babysit her four nieces while Claudia and her husband went for a rare evening out.

'You know Mother,' Mornay said lightly, and was then slightly startled to find herself under Claudia's scrutiny.

'Why don't you leave?' her sister asked bluntly.

'It's not so bad.'

'Yes, it is, it's dreadful. For goodness' sake, I'd left home two years by the time I was your age!'

'But——'

'But nothing,' Claudia said crossly, and pressed on, 'What with your fantastic skin and your gorgeous blonde hair, not to mention your terrific big blue eyes, you're absolutely stunning, Mornay. No way should you be spending your Saturday nights babysitting, but with Mother and Father certain you'll come to a bad end "like your sister" and making you nervous to take home any gutsy flesh and blood male—not that I'd bother letting them vet my dates anyway——' she inserted hotly '—you might just as well start now to take a liking to knitting and stray cats.'

'What's wrong with knitting and stray cats?' Gerry Overton asked as he came into the room at the tail-end of what his wife was saying.

'Claudia's having a "go" at me,' Mornay told him, genuinely fond of her tall and thin shaggy-bearded brother-in-law who adored her sister.

'You know you're more than welcome to move in here any time it gets too much for you,' he told her seriously.

'Thanks, Gerry,' Mornay smiled, but she knew she would stay put.

'You're too soft,' Claudia told her. And life had gone on much the same for another year, the only difference being that occasionally in that year Mornay had experienced the stirrings of something akin to a feeling that she would not mind moving into a place of her own.

During that year, though, she had started going out occasionally with Robert Naylor. Robert was kind to old ladies and dumb animals, was keen on bird-watching—and was never going to set the world on fire. Mornay knew within half an hour of her first date with him any vital chemistry that would make them more than 'just good friends' was lacking. But, since Robert wasn't pushy and didn't want to be forever attempting to kiss her or hold her hand, he became her most regular boyfriend.

It was a bonus that her parents liked him, Mornay thought, and came out of her reverie to realise that she was locking the door to her flat and was on her way to work. She went down the stairs to the outer door, musing that she must have eaten her breakfast and, out of habit, tidied her flat and rinsed her cup, saucer and plate, all without knowing it.

As she walked over to the area where she garaged her car, however, her thoughts went back to how her parents' liking Robert had come in very useful when two years ago her father had been offered promotion which he felt he would be a fool to turn down. The only snag was that he would have to leave Reefingham in order to be within much easier commuting distance to his head office.

'There's nothing for it, my dear,' he had addressed his wife over the dinner table, 'we'll have to sell up and look for something nearer to Birmingham.'

'I rather fancy Solihull,' Dorothy Haynes had replied. 'Is Solihull close enough to Birmingham?'

Mornay was a quiet third at the table while Solihull was discussed. She knew that she would have to make the move with them, but knew also that, while she had nothing against Solihull, she wanted to stay in

Reefingham near to her sister, in whose erratic household she had known innocent fun and laughter.

'You're very quiet, Mornay!' Fifteen minutes into the conversation Dorothy Haynes suddenly noticed that her younger offspring had said not a word. 'Oh!' she then said, and, as though something had just occurred to her, 'I see,' she had gone on, and then, making Mornay stare at her wide-eyed, 'You don't want to come with us, do you?'

'I...' Mornay murmured, a feeling welling up in her that she must tell her parents exactly how she felt, but, against that, years of experience warning that if she didn't want her parents going on at her endlessly that she was going to turn out just like her sister, she had better stay quiet. Suddenly then, though, she grabbed at a strand of courage. 'I——' she began.

'Of course she wants to come with us, my dear,' Mornay's father interrupted when she had been on the brink of hauling down coals of wrath upon her head. 'Don't you, Mornay?'

Strangely, though, Mornay found that she had a streak of stubbornness in her. At any rate, she discovered that, whatever the outcome, whatever the extent of the verbal battering she might be letting herself in for, something in her was refusing this time meekly to acquiesce. Suddenly she was discovering that her 'anything for a quiet life' view of the past was starting to splinter.

'I—wouldn't mind—er—staying on in Reefingham,' she actually heard her own voice speak up.

'What did you say?' her father demanded heavily.

But before she could discover whether or not she had the courage to repeat it, her mother was putting a quick two and two together, and coming up with a totally erroneous five. 'Robert Naylor,' she announced to her husband.

'Robert N——' he repeated. Whether the fact that she had been dating Robert for a year now had been discussed by her parents, Mornay didn't know. But it seemed that her father was making the same error as her mother when he caught on. Mornay was little short of astonished however when, just as if she weren't there, he told her mother, 'Well, Robert won't be in a position to marry for a few years yet,' and, as she stared at her parents in amazement, the subject of the Solihull move was temporarily abandoned while they discussed Robert Naylor's prospects. Some while later, with Mornay having taken no part in the discussion, her parents had magnanimously agreed that, if a suitable apartment could be found for her in Reefingham, then if she really did not wish to move with them she could stay behind.

Hardly able to believe that her heart's desire looked like being achieved without an uphill battle where she would be shown up to be the most ungrateful daughter ever born, Mornay could see no point in ruining everything by telling her parents that she had no intention whatsoever of marrying Robert Naylor. Though while part of her was convinced that this way a lot of unnecessary fuss and bother could be avoided, there was another part which felt dreadfully guilty that—without his knowledge—she had used Robert so.

Which, she thought as she headed her Austin Metro towards the Town Hall that Monday morning, was probably why two years later she was still dating him.

Her thoughts were not upon Robert Naylor, nor her parents as she parked her car, swung into the Town Hall, and made for her office. They were on her sister, who was expecting her fifth child in a couple of weeks, and on how she did not suppose another little Overton in the scatty household was going to make it any less scatty.

There was a smile on her beautiful mouth as she reflected that, however frenetic, even mad sometimes that household appeared after her sedate upbringing, it seemed always, again unlike the home she and Claudia were brought up in, to be filled with love and laughter.

'How you can look so cheerful on a Monday morning beats me!' her nice and safe boss greeted her.

'Good morning, Mr Probert,' she replied, and smiled still. 'It's the weather,' she told him.

They discussed the present heatwave and the fact that, though May had been one of the wettest on record, another week of the hot, dry weather was bound to coincide with calls to conserve water. They then got down to work.

It was around mid-morning that a call came through that was nothing to do with work. 'Surveyor's Department,' Mornay answered the phone.

'It's me—Gerry,' the caller identified himself.

'Everything all right?' Mornay asked him. He sounded on top of the world, but it was more usually Claudia who rang her if she wanted her to babysit—not that she could see her wanting to go anywhere, with the baby due so soon.

'Couldn't be better!' Gerry cried exuberantly. 'I've got a *son*!'

'A son! But Claudia——!'

Over the next few minutes her brother-in-law related how, not waiting for two weeks, things had started to happen in the early hours, and how he'd phoned his father to drive his mother over to stay with Emily, Alice, Florence and Prudence while he'd driven Claudia to Reefingham General. Half an hour ago she had presented him with the son he had always secretly wanted.

'She's all right—and the baby?' Mornay asked urgently, feeling weepy but doing her best not to give way in the office.

'Fine—both of them,' Gerry assured her. 'You should see him,' he went charging on. 'Red face, red hair and—like his dad—handsome.'

'Clown,' Mornay laughed, and felt better and less like crying as she asked when could she go and see her sister.

'She's coming out of hospital tomorrow, but I'm sure she'd love to have a visit from you tonight,' Gerry told her.

'You don't mind?' she enquired, wanting quite badly to be at the maternity wing of Reefingham General that night, but not wanting to encroach on this special visiting time between husband and wife.

'Dope!' Gerry scoffed. 'My mother's staying with the girls all day, so I'm free to visit this afternoon *and* this evening.' He rang off, clearly overjoyed that the son he wanted was his.

'Do I gather from what I've overheard that you're an aunt again?' Mr Probert broke through the haze of Mornay's thought to enquire jovially.

'Isn't it super?' she beamed.

It crossed through her mind that she ought to ring her mother and pass on the glad tidings. The thought, however, that her mother would most likely shudder and look on Claudia's new infant more as her daughter bringing a fifth unruly monster into the world made Mornay decide that relating the news could wait until lunchtime.

Dorothy Haynes' reception of the news of her fifth grandchild was much as Mornay had expected when at a quarter past one she stood in a public telephone booth and made the connection to Solihull. Though it was fair to say that, even though her parents had—for the look of it—unbent sufficiently to attend Claudia's wedding nine and a half years ago, there had been little love lost between them since the day Claudia had left home. Which made it fairly predictable, Mornay realised, that instead of asking after mother and baby her mother's first comment was, 'It's to be hoped that she doesn't have any more!'

'Actually, I think both Claudia and Gerry like large families,' Mornay said on a flicker of anger. And, rather surprised at what was, for her, something of an outburst,

'I'm seeing Claudia tonight—can I give her a message from you?'

'I'll write to her when I have a moment,' her mother replied stiffly.

Mornay said goodbye and felt quite cross with her mother. She doubted then that her parents had ever loved either her or her sister. Normal parents, normal loving parents, would not talk in terms of writing but, she felt, in terms of getting to see the mother and new babe as soon as they could.

Mornay was busy that afternoon and was up to her eyes in work when she received her second personal call of the day. This time it was Robert Naylor.

'I'm afraid I'll have to cancel seeing you tomorrow night,' he apologised straight away.

It was on the tip of Mornay's tongue to quip, 'You love another?' but she knew Robert would think that she had gone crazy. 'Oh?' she murmured, wondering what on earth had got into her today. She had awakened contented, which mood had quickly changed to being dissatisfied, and she had mulled darkly over the repressions of her childhood which had seemed to be following her into adult life. She had then felt momentarily anxious over Claudia, and then tearful and then, for a rarity, she had felt angry with her mother *and* had let it show. She was not certain when so many moods and emotions had visited her all in the space of eight hours. 'You're off somewhere?' she guessed. Robert worked as a peripatetic stock-controller for a wallpaper combine, and visited most corners of the British Isles during the course of his work.

'I have to go to Wales at short notice,' he told her importantly. 'I may not be back before Friday.'

'I'll see you when you return, then,' Mornay answered non-committally and, because she knew more eagerness to see her new nephew than 'nice and safe' Robert, 'Don't forget to take your field glasses,' she injected some warmth into her voice to tell him. 'You might be able to fit in some bird-watching while you're away.'

'I always have my binoculars in the car, you know that,' he replied.

Mornay sat staring into space for some minutes after she had put the phone down. She owned then that she was feeling—and it had been coming on for some time, she acknowledged—a bit fed up with Robert. How, though, she went on to wonder, did one end a three-year relationship without causing hurt? Relationship, though, was hardly the word to use for the tepid sort of friendship she had going with Robert. And would he be hurt anyway? Did she even want to finish with him? What was there to finish, for goodness' sake? He was more like a brother than a lover. The thought of having Robert for a lover, though, was laughable. Yet she didn't want to hurt him.

Why, she began to wonder as she got on with some work, had she started to think in terms of telling Robert that she wouldn't see him any more? Unable to find an answer, she put the vagaries of her moods that day down to the heatwave that was at present scorching the country and absorbed herself in that which she was paid to do.

Back at her flat that early evening, she had a quick shower, a quick bite of something to eat and was dressed in a fresh summer dress with plenty of time to spare in which to get to the hospital.

That was, she did have plenty of time to spare until suddenly the phone rang to announce her agitated brother-in-law. 'Can you come and pick me up?' he asked urgently. 'Now, of all times, my car won't start. I'd ask Dad to run me to the hospital but it would take longer for him to get here than you.'

'I'm on my way,' Mornay told him, having quickly assessed the situation and anxious to get started so that they would not be late for the visiting period allowed.

Gerry, his mother and Emily, Alice, Florence and Prudence were all in the garden that ran along one side of the big old house when Mornay, the magazines she had brought for Claudia on the seat beside her, pulled up a short while later and got out of the car.

'Hello, Mornay,' Mrs Overton greeted her, looking strained as she came over to the three-foot-high hedge. 'It's ages since I last saw you—how are you?' she asked warmly.

'Fine, thank you, Mrs Overton,' Mornay smiled. 'Hello, girls,' she greeted the four who came tearing over, but anything else she might have said was lost when Gerry, clearly in a hurry, took a short-cut across the lawn and, charging out of the gate, held his hands out for her car keys.

'You can have a natter with Mornay when we get back,' Gerry told his mother when, knowing of old that her brother-in-law had a 'thing' about being driven by a woman, Mornay, in this instance of him being uptight about the possibility of keeping his wife waiting, handed over her car keys.

They drove off to the sound of Mrs Overton's, 'Really! The responsibilities of parenthood haven't improved your manners any, young man!'

When, having calmed down considerably, Gerry later relayed his panic of the last hour to his wife, Claudia broke up in giggles. 'Young man!' she hooted. 'Lord, I bet that pleased you. You haven't been "young man" since you were twenty and were carpeted by your father for having made me pregnant.'

'He did cut up a bit rough,' Gerry recalled. 'He's got a meeting tonight so he'll call to pick Mother up around ten.'

'Talking of mothers, did you ring mine, Mornay?' Claudia turned to ask her sister.

'I did, and...'

'And?' Claudia prompted.

'And she was very pleased about your news, and she's going to write to you, and she sent her love...'

'And you are the rottenest liar I've ever come across.'

'Have you decided on what to call the little chap?' Mornay abruptly changed the conversation, and Claudia looked to Gerry.

'I like the name Luke,' she told him.

'Which reminds me, if you'll excuse me, ladies, that it's about time I went and took a look at Master Luke Overton, my son,' Gerry said proudly, and with a peck on his wife's cheek he went from the ward.

Mornay would have liked to have gone to see baby Luke herself, but she sensed that Claudia, for all she wasn't showing it, was feeling a shade hurt that her mother cared so little that she could not be bothered to come and see her. Now, Mornay felt, was not the time to leave Claudia on her own.

'Are they really letting you home tomorrow?' she asked brightly.

'They'd better,' Claudia grinned. 'They only wanted me to come while I had Luke just in case of complications. Gerry, as you know, is having a couple of weeks off, so between us we'll soon have ourselves in some sort of routine.'

'Are you serious?' Mornay asked her, Claudia's household, even without the new babe, being the most disorganised she could imagine.

'Oh, shut up,' Claudia said rudely, and grinned, and they were both in happy humour when Gerry, cock-a-hoop after seeing his son, came back.

A little while later Mornay said goodbye to her sister and, leaving Gerry so that he could have some private time with his wife, she went out to the hospital car park. Only when she approached her car and made as though to take the car keys from her bag did she realise that Gerry still had them.

Still, it was a warm evening, not to say airless, and she would most probably have chosen to wait for him outside the car anyway.

Gerry was beaming from ear to ear when he eventually joined Mornay—a very different person from the tense and anxious not to be late person he had been earlier.

'Let's go and wet the baby's head!' he suggested as soon as he had let her into her car and had positioned himself behind the driving-wheel.

'Your mother will be waiting,' Mornay pointed out, aware that Gerry, understandably perhaps, was in a state of euphoria, but not wanting to be late if his daughters— who'd never heard of strict bedtime—were wearing their grandmother out.

'Your upbringing's showing,' her brother-in-law jibed teasingly.

'So mine's a half,' Mornay told him, realising that in the circumstances she was being extremely stuffy.

The sky had darkened and the heat was oppressive when, limiting 'wetting the baby's head' to one drink, they left the pub.

'We're going to have a thunderstorm,' Mornay said as Gerry turned on the headlights and steered the car out of the car park.

'Who cares?' he sang as he put his foot down and negotiated his way towards the centre of town prior to taking the road that led to Penny Dale.

Mornay smiled affectionately as she saw the traffic-light they were nearing change to amber. She was beginning to wonder if her brother-in-law would ever come down to earth again when, as the traffic-light changed to red, she saw a tall dark-haired man step from the pavement. He looked straight at them, and as his aristocratic features registered in her head—without her being fully aware of it—all thought in her suddenly ceased as she realised that Gerry was not going to stop!

'Slow down—brake!' she cried sharply. But it was too late!

The car lurched violently as Gerry suddenly became aware of what was happening and hit the brakes while at the same time he spun the steering-wheel frantically in a vain effort to avoid hitting the tall pedestrian. Mornay hung on as she saw the man collapse to the ground and the car lurched from left to right, thudded against a bollard, and bounced back to the road again.

By that time, though, they were halfway across the intersection. But to her astonishment, even as she unfastened her seatbelt and placed a hand on the doorhandle ready to go sprinting back to the injured man, Gerry was suddenly accelerating away.

'*Stop!*' she shrieked as, thrown back in her seat, she realised that he couldn't have seen the man collapse. 'We've knocked someone over!'

Her astonishment was total when, with a glance in his rear-view mirror, Gerry, instead of halting, kept his foot down and replied, 'He'll be all right. There's quite a crowd of people round him, they'll see to him.'

'But we have to stop!' Mornay told him forcefully. 'We might have killed him or something.'

'Grief, Mornay, I only tapped him—don't be so dramatic,' Gerry snapped, but he sounded all at once very agitated, and she formed a clear impression that he was trying to convince himself as much as her that he had only 'tapped' the accident victim.

He was turning on to the Penny Dale road, away from the direction of the nearest police station by then, but whether he was in a state of agitation or not Mornay felt she could do no other than remind him, 'We'll have to report it to the police, Gerry.'

'Don't you dare!' he replied, and sounded as shaken as she felt.

'But, Gerry, we——'

'Dammit, Mornay, I've enough points against me for silly driving offences—I'll lose my licence for sure if I have to go to court over this one!'

She had known that he had been caught for speeding a couple of times, and had last year been in a spot of bother for a small traffic accident, but in her view none of his previous traffic misdemeanours compared with the enormity of what had just happened.

'But you can't pretend it just—never happened,' she protested. 'It——'

'I can if it comes to a battle between my conscience about knocking a bloke over who in all probability was only stunned for a minute and then got up and walked away—and knowing that if I reported it, then my wife—*your sister*—can say goodbye to any feeling of security that I provide.'

'Why should doing what's right affect Claudia's security?' Mornay asked him sharply.

Gerry spent the time until they reached his home in telling her just how Claudia's security would be affected. He worked in the building industry as a site inspector, and it was his job to go around to any new building being erected to check that work was being completed to specification. A vehicle and a licence to drive were essential to his work, he highlighted. If he lost his licence and was banned from driving, he could say goodbye to his job and his wife and children could say goodbye to the standard of living which they now enjoyed.

'I can't do it to her, Mornay,' Gerry told her shakily as he pulled up outside his home. 'I've seen other women bowed down with worry about how they're going to feed their growing kids. I don't want that for my Claudia. And I'm sure you don't either.'

'Of course I don't. But . . .'

'Can't you see how idiotic you're being, love?' he asked. 'I'm sure that fellow's all right. Is it worth ruining your sister's happiness just because you've a nuisance of a conscience? You saw how happy she was tonight,' he applied more pressure. 'Could you bear to see her worn down with worry and unhappy?'

When it was put like that, Mornay supposed she was being idiotic. 'Are you going to tell your mother what happened?'

'I'm telling no one,' he answered.

It was no surprise to Mornay that she did not sleep well that night. Back in her flat, she went to bed with the accident to the forefront of her mind and lay awake for an age. When she did sleep, however, it was to be brief and she was to awaken at three in the morning from the most horrendous nightmare where she, at the wheel of her car, had shot the traffic lights and had mown down Claudia.

The sound of her own scream brought Mornay out of her nightmare. Bathed in perspiration, she got out of bed and went to the kitchen. She made a pot of tea and, feeling most disinclined to return to her bed, she sat for an age trying to get the nightmare out of her head. It was only natural that she should dream so violently, she mused shakily, and tried to put out of her mind the insistent prod of a thought that maybe her awful dream was meant to symbolise that she held Claudia's life in her hands. That should she follow the dictates of her conscience and report the accident, then, through her, Claudia's happy life would be over.

By the time Mornay returned to her bed an hour later, she knew that she was going to have to learn to live with her conscience. Claudia and her happiness were paramount.

Strangely, though, when Mornay lay down and closed her eyes, it was not the face of her sister that floated before her, but the face of a tall, dark stranger. A man she had never seen before that night, but a man whose strong, aristocratic features she suddenly had the most uncanny feeling that she would never forget.

When Mornay awakened from another restless sleep at six o'clock she was instantly wide awake and of the belief that it was not uncanny at all that she should feel she would never forget that man's face. She was of the opinion then that, in view of his having been knocked off his feet by her car, it would be most surprising if she *had* forgotten his face.

She sighed unhappily as she showered and dressed and hoped with all her heart that, as Gerry had suggested, the man had got up and walked away.

Proof, however, that the man had not 'got up and walked away' came when, with ages to go before she need leave for work, Mornay went over to her radio and twiddled the knobs until she was tuned into her local radio station. Tension began to mount in her while she waited for the disc being played to end. And then the announcer was saying, 'And now for some local news. Police are still looking for the hit-and-run driver who knocked over a man in Reefingham High Street around nine o'clock last night.' Her throat went dry as she sank soundlessly down on to a chair. 'Witnesses have described the vehicle as being brown or green and as being either a Ford Fiesta or a Vauxhall Astra.' Mornay was sitting gripping hard on to the sides of her chair, she and her brother-in-law alone knowing that the car involved had been a maroon Austin Metro, when the announcer came to the most important part as far as she was concerned. 'The injured man was taken to Reefingham General, where his condition was said to be comfortable half an hour ago.' Mornay was hovering between thanking God that Gerry hadn't killed him, and anxiety that even so the man had landed up in hospital when, to make her blood go cold, the announcer added,

'Unfortunately, when the hit-and-run victim regained consciousness, he was found to have lost his memory.'

Lost his memory! 'Oh, no!' Mornay gasped out loud. Stunned, she sat staring, horrified, at the radio. Oh, no, the poor, poor man!

CHAPTER TWO

MORNAY was still sitting in stunned silence, knowing in her heart of hearts that she was going to have to contact the police, when her telephone rang. Switching off the radio as she went, she ran into a towering wall of guilt when, wondering who could be ringing her at this early hour, she realised that it must be Claudia.

She picked up the phone, fully expecting to hear her sister giving forth on the unseemingly hour one was awakened in hospital, only to hear that it was not Claudia who was calling but her husband.

'I've just tuned in to the local radio station,' he began without preamble, 'and——'

'I caught the local news too,' Mornay told him flatly. 'So you know...?'

'Yes, I know,' Mornay told him, and, guessing why he was ringing—or so she thought, 'I'd better call in at the police station on my way to work. Do you want to meet me there?'

'Are you off your head?' Gerry exclaimed urgently. 'For pity's sake, Mornay, we had all this out last night! You agreed then that we could do nothing if we didn't want to jeopardise Claudia's happiness.'

'I know,' Mornay admitted, feeling miserable. 'But that was before I heard the news just now. The poor man didn't walk away from the accident but landed up in hospital without a clue to who he is, and...and it would be criminal for us not to...'

'It would be more criminal to let your sister and her babies suffer just because you've got a fidgety conscience!' Gerry declared, his alarm obvious. 'Would it

25

make your conscience feel any better to know that through you my family will suffer?'

'No,' she said unhappily, and heard Gerry go on for another five minutes much in the same vein as the previous evening.

'They said on the radio that the man was comfortable, so he's not in a bad way,' Gerry came to an end. 'And you aren't going to make his memory return by going to the police and letting me in for a load of grief, are you?'

'No,' Mornay had to allow, but she felt her guilt no easier to live with after he had rung off, even if he did make it sound as though it would be a far bigger crime to report that her car had been anywhere in the vicinity of the High Street last night.

By the time she left her flat that morning Mornay had again managed to see the situation in the same light as her brother-in-law. That, however, did not make her feel in any way less jumpy. By the sound of it the police were looking for either an Astra or a Fiesta but, as she went to get her car out of its garage, she felt it would be some time before she would pass a policeman in the street without squirming.

Dismay hit her with a vengeance when, having reversed her car out of the garage, she went back to close the garage doors. There for all the world to see was a dent the size of a man's fist on the offside wing. Even without the dent, the fact that some of the maroon paintwork seemed to be missing struck fear into her heart. For certain daylight would reveal traces of maroon—not brown or green—paint left behind on the bollard her Metro had tangled with last night! Mornay drove her car back into its garage and decided to walk to work.

She had no sooner got to work however, than Gerry was on the phone to speak to her again. 'I haven't changed my mind,' she told him, while appreciating his nervousness, not really wanting him to ring her every five minutes of the day.

'I'm not ringing about that,' he told her. 'I've just rung the hospital to see what time I can collect Claudia, and they've said that she can't come home today.'

Immediately Mornay's heart lurched in panic. 'Why not? What's wrong with her?' she questioned quickly.

'Nothing to be too alarmed about, apparently,' Gerry quickly assured her. 'It's just that her temperature's rocketed for some reason, and they're insisting that she stays put until it comes down. Why I'm ringing, more particularly, is that my mother was a bit miffed as you know last night that the kids had been playing up, so I don't like to ask her to sit with them again so soon. Could you come and sit with them tonight for me while I go and visit Claudia?'

'Of course I will,' Mornay told him. 'Oh,' she suddenly remembered, 'have you got transport?'

She put the phone down having heard that Gerry had already had his car looked at and that the problem was nothing more serious than petrol pump failure, which had not taken long to sort out.

An involuntary sigh escaped Mornay as she got on with some work. 'Everything all right?' Mr Probert enquired.

She wished very much that she could confide in him, though knew that if she did he would only advise her to do what she knew she ought to do anyway. 'Claudia was supposed to be coming out of hospital today but her temperature's soared so they're keeping her in,' she told him by way of explanation for the fact that she was finding it very hard to find a smile that day.

'She'll be all right,' Mr Probert replied warmly. 'And she really is in the best place if she's not feeling quite up to the mark.'

'You're right, of course,' Mornay agreed, and spent the next couple of hours telling herself that, as he'd said, of course Claudia would be all right, and wondering whether she would, and what the penalty was for trying to cover up a hit-and-run crime.

She had worked herself up into a state where she was convinced that the next person who came through the office door would be a uniformed officer to ask if she was the owner of a maroon-coloured car, when the door suddenly opened. The person who came in, though uniformed, was not a policeman, but the commissionaire bringing a hand-delivered package. It was he, however, who brought the news that there had been a hold-up in one of the banks in the main street, and so unwittingly gave Mornay a very small modicum of ease in the tension she was enduring.

Surely a bank raid would have the local constabulary using all their resources in chasing after the bank robbers! The police were always short-staffed—weren't they? And if they weren't—it went without saying that a bank robbery would take priority over a hit-and-run episode where no one had been seriously hurt!

Within minutes she was feeling dreadful again. That poor man! She tried to visualise losing her memory and thought it must be utterly ghastly. If he didn't know who he was, then the hospital couldn't know who he was, and the police couldn't know who he was—and that meant that they couldn't tell anyone *where* he was.

Mornay went out on her lunch-break but felt too churned up inside to be able to eat. That poor man, his wife wouldn't know where he was, there'd be no one to visit him—oh, how desperate he must be feeling!

She returned to her office feeling bodily weary from her lack of sleep last night and mentally used up from constantly having her mind on Claudia, the accident, and the injured man.

Unbeknown to her, however, she had made several mistakes in her work that day and, because this was such an unusual occurrence, Mr Probert came from his office to see her. She was staring into space when at around half-past two she became aware that her boss was standing at her desk.

'This...' he began, indicating some typing she had done and which he now held. Then he paused, and, giving her unsmiling expression a searching look, he changed what he had been about to say to tell her kindly, 'Why don't you take an hour off and go and visit your sister to see for yourself that she's all right?'

Mornay averted her eyes as it dawned on her that the anxiety she was going through must be showing. 'It's all right,' she mumbled, and experienced more guilt—this time at Mr Probert's misplaced kindness.

'Do me a favour,' he smiled, and, tapping the papers in his hands, 'Your work's suffering.'

'Oh, I'm sorry,' Mornay immediately apologised, and reached for her bag. Perhaps a visit to Claudia might endorse for her that by keeping quiet she was doing only what was right. 'I'll work late tonight,' she told Mr Probert as she got to her feet, and was stepping out the half-mile to Reefingham General before she recalled that she was babysitting that night. She'd have to go home for her car first, and if she wasn't at Claudia's house by a quarter to seven then Gerry would start to flap.

Realising that she'd have to back-track on her offer to work late, Mornay made a mental promise to work hard and pay closer attention to detail, and stopped by the hospital gates where an enterprising lady had set up a flower stall.

'I'll have two bunches of the red carnations, please,' she requested, thinking the bright colour would cheer Claudia up if she was down in the doldrums.

Having made her purchase, Mornay went through the main gates and up the drive of the hospital and through the main doors. Over the years she had become familiar with where each department lay, having at some time or another made a visit to someone or other in the various wards.

Apart from her visit last evening to the maternity wing—where Claudia had been delivered of her five babies—Mornay had many years previously visited the accident wing when Gerry—in those days the owner of a motorbike—had fallen off it.

She had no intention of visiting the accident wing, though. Indeed, had she thought about it, she would have determined to give that particular wing a very wide berth. But she suddenly discovered that, without any known volition, instead of turning right at the end of the long corridor, she had turned left. More, that in finding her feet were taking her along to the accident wing, she didn't seem able to stop.

Abruptly, as if to prove herself wrong, Mornay halted. Yet, having done that, there seemed to be someone else in charge of her, in that she found herself thinking that it wouldn't hurt at all if she went along to Sister's office to enquire how the man was whom she'd heard on the news had lost his memory. Slowly, as though compelled, Mornay resumed walking.

She knew where the ward sister's office was. The wards in this old building were all laid out pretty much the same, with double swing doors leading to another set of double swing doors. In between the two sets of doors, though, lay—to one side—a small kitchen, a walk-in linen cupboard and a side-ward big enough for two beds. Opposite lay a bathroom, a place where wheelchairs were generally parked and Sister's office, which had a window in it which looked on to the ward.

Pushing her way quietly through the first set of swing doors, Mornay took a few paces forward and was able to see through the glass of the other swing doors that it was visiting time, and that relatives and friends were seated by the various beds. Quickly she averted her eyes. The face of the man Gerry had knocked down seemed to be burned into her brain. She had enough guilt to be going on with without recognising him—or the fact that his would be the only bed without a visitor.

Nevertheless, she somehow still felt unable to go from the place where her feet had taken her, and she moved to where she knew she would find the ward sister, and tapped gently on the door. She then followed through by reaching for the door-handle, and turned it. She then took a step or two forward and stepped round the door— and knew, instantly, that she had made the most terrible mistake!

Sister's office must be on the other side of the connecting passageway. She, Mornay saw as she fought to hold down a sudden surge of panic, had entered a side-ward—a side-ward which had only one occupant, who was a man she would know anywhere! A man who, for all he was lying down in bed, she knew to be tall. A man who looked to be somewhere in his mid-thirties, and who had dark hair and aristocratic features—and whose dark eyes, as she nervously eyed him, were lazily assessing her.

'Come in,' he invited in unhurried tones.

He had a pleasant-sounding voice, she thought, but she was more inclined to make a hasty exit rather than go any closer to him. Then it was that she noticed that, although the man seemed to be free of bandages or plaster, there was an extreme look of exhaustion about him. Then it was that her conscience awakened with a vengeance and, as she saw how, all because of his having made contact with her car, his face was drained of colour and that he looked worn out, she could no more leave than fly.

'How are you feeling?' she asked, and so that he should not have to strain any sore muscles by turning to look at her she moved closer to him.

'There have been days when I've felt better,' he drawled in reply.

'Did you break any bones—or anything?' she wanted to know.

Relief started to rush in when he moved his head slightly from side to side in a negative reply. Then, 'Pull up a chair,' he invited.

As Mornay had had no intention of going any further into the room, she had no intention of pulling up a chair either. But, as her eyes again examined the exhausted-looking man, so she became guiltily aware that it might be causing him some effort to look up to where she was standing.

Hurriedly she found a chair and carried it to the bed. They were then on more of a level as she sat by the side of his bed. Suddenly though, as she became aware of his steady dark-eyed stare fixed on her features, Mornay all at once found that she was hurrying into a rapid false explanation of why she was there.

'I thought I'd come and see if there is anything you need,' she lied.

'You're some sort of voluntary worker?' he enquired.

'Oh, no, I'm a secretary,' she heard herself confess, and then, knowing full well that she hadn't much of a clue when it came to telling lies, she realised that if her innate honesty was not going to trip her up she would do well to think carefully over every word she uttered during what she was going to make the briefest ever visit. 'It was just that...' She hesitated and, having been about to tell him that she had heard about his accident on the radio that morning, she realised that that could get her into the realms of what sort of vehicle had hit him—a discussion on which was something she was anxious to avoid. 'It was just that—I was walking in the High Street last night when I saw the ambulance come and take you away.'

Hoping that her face did not look as pink as it felt, Mornay just then observed that, for all the man looked drained of strength, an alert sort of look had suddenly come to his eyes. She couldn't remember seeing it there before, at any rate.

His tone was easy, though, when he enquired mildly, 'You witnessed the accident?'

'Oh, no!' Mornay straight away denied any such idea, and, wanting to get him swiftly away from the notion, 'I arrived just in time to see the ambulance take you away, and today——'

'From what I hear,' the man butted in to remark, 'that ambulance broke all speed records to get me here without a moment's delay.'

'The ambulance driver didn't hang about, certainly,' she smiled, and, since someone must have told him of the speed and efficiency of their local ambulance service, 'No sooner were the rear doors closed than he was away,' she added for a touch of authenticity. Then she resumed, 'I was passing the hospital today, and——'

'You don't perform your secretarial duties on Tuesdays?' he interrupted her to question, and Mornay knew then that she had better tread very carefully. This man might be physically debilitated, but his brain was as sharp as a tack.

'I'm having an hour off—to go to the dentist,' she of the perfect teeth lied, and quickly took up again, 'When I was passing the hospital and I remembered the incident of last night, I wondered if—that is, if your—er—family—weren't able to—er...' She was floundering, and she knew it. She still felt that she had to keep quiet about having heard on the radio that morning the report which mentioned not only the speculation about the vehicle in question, but also his loss of memory. But added to that was an inner sensitivity she felt to the distress he must be suffering on account of his lost memory, and she just could not go on to make further reference to his family.

To her relief, he saved her from having to stammer on when, with a smile of some charm, he suddenly seemed to notice the red carnations she was clutching.

'You brought these for me?' he enquired.

Claudia, the intended recipient, was far from Mornay's mind when, in her relief, she grabbed at the suggestion. 'I thought they might cheer you up if you were feeling down,' she smiled in return, and got so far carried away that she began earnestly, 'If there's anything you need,' when he gritted one short and angry word that had her staring at him, wide-eyed. 'What...?' she asked, certain, for all there was no trace of a smile about him now, charming or otherwise, that she must have heard him incorrectly.

But she had not heard him incorrectly, she discovered. For he repeated that word again. 'Liar,' he gritted, 'was what I called you—and not a very good liar at that!'

'I ... What ...?' She struggled for a moment or two under his dark, forbidding stare. Then, as her common logic assessed that he could not possibly know the extent of her lies, she realised that his comment must have been made in connection with the flowers she had just said she'd brought him. 'I know some men don't appreciate flowers,' she surfaced to find a smile, 'but—— '

'Since it's through you that I'm cooped up in this damned place and likely to be for some days,' he cut her off harshly, 'to bring flowers is——'

'Through me!' Mornay choked on a whisper, fear entering her heart when, her brain seeming to seize up, she swallowed on a dry throat. With nothing very clever coming to her numbed brain, however, she could only attempt to bluff. 'I don't know what you're talking about,' she said and, trying for an aloof note, 'How on earth could I possibly have anything to do with you being—er...' her aloof manner started to slip under his harsh glare '...hospitalised?' she managed to finish.

'I'll tell you how,' he snarled, and did not waste any time in doing so. 'For starters, you weren't *walking* in the area of the High Street last night, you were driving! For——'

'Don't be absurd!' Mornay, inwardly in utter panic, tried to cut in.

'Nor were you paying proper attention to your driving,' he ignored her to rap.

'I always pay proper attention to my driving,' Mornay told him coldly, and could have groaned out loud when she realised that she would have been better to tell him that she did not drive at all.

'Which is why you shot a red light, hit me, and then, criminally, without stopping, drove on—is it?' he barked.

Mornay opened her mouth to hotly deny it. But then, suddenly, she was startled into realising that it was *her* he was accusing! All at once, it dawned on her that this man—having not so much as an idea that she had a brother-in-law, thought that it had been *her* at the steering-wheel of the car that had hit him last evening! Swiftly Mornay recalled the blue funk which Gerry had been in last night. Swiftly, too, she recalled all the arguments he had used for why she should stay quiet. And swiftly it came to her that, even though this man, despite looking as though to sleep for a week might do him some good, had still retained quite brilliant powers of deduction to have worked out what he so far had— Gerry might still get away with it!

Realising that she had been silent too long to make any scornful denial sound genuine, Mornay felt she had better hop on to the attack. 'You can't prove that statement,' she shrugged, hoping to convey that she did not believe him to be seriously accusing her anyway.

But, to make her insides churn with another helping of panic, 'I just did!' he grated acidly, and as Mornay's grasp of the flowers she still held tightened convulsively, he seemed about to add more acid when the door suddenly opened.

Her heart went into her mouth when she saw from the navy dress and white-bibbed apron that the person who had just come in was the ward sister. Only then did

Mornay realise that she must have secretly been hoping to leave the side-ward with no one being any wiser about her visit.

The plump ward sister was frowning severely though, Mornay observed as her heart plummeted to her boots and she realised that the man in the bed would lose no time in acquainting the nursing sister with his suspicions.

'Who——?' the ward sister began to demand, and Mornay had visions of being physically held down by the tough-looking lady if need be, while the police were called.

But no, to her surprise, not to say utmost gratitude, the man in the bed was suddenly cutting through whatever the sister would have said. 'Don't be starchy, Sister,' he smiled, the charm which Mornay had observed in him before—phoney charm, she now realised—there again. But, while she still expected him to repeat his allegations to the plump woman, 'I'm sure you wouldn't deprive me of my beautiful visitor.'

Mornay instantly switched her gaze from the sister to the man in the bed. She felt confused suddenly that the man who but a minute earlier had been all aggression, should a minute later describe her as beautiful and sound as though he meant it. Nor did her confusion end there. She was still trying to get to grips with the confusing fact that it looked as though he might keep his suspicions to himself when, having glanced back to the woman who had just come in, she saw the sister's look of curiosity to know who she was fade under her professional concern for her patient.

'You're supposed to be kept quiet,' she told him succinctly. And then, as though begrudgingly, 'Five minutes!' she allowed.

'If you're to be kept quiet...' Mornay murmured as soon as the sister had gone. In the next moment, she was on her feet.

Astonishingly, however, and with lightning speed, and all before she had taken so much as half a step away from the bed, his right hand had snaked out and had taken hold of her wrist in a grip there was no shaking off.

Mornay was still staring in amazement that a man who looked so drained of vitality should have such quick reactions and such strength when, 'Your visit isn't over yet,' he stated laconically.

Again her heart plummeted. But she took hope from the fact that he had not revealed his suspicions to the ward sister when she had been there. The same ward sister, she recalled without effort, had allowed five minutes' visiting time only. Surely she could find something to talk about in the time remaining before that fierce-looking woman came and insisted that, for the good of her patient, she must go.

Alas, the very thing which Mornay had not meant to refer to was the first thing that rolled off her tongue. 'Do you know who you are yet?' she found herself enquiring, and, wishing that the floor would open up beneath her, she felt impelled to gently go on, 'Have you recovered your memory?' His answer had her staring at him incredulously.

'I never lost it!' he announced forthrightly, and while she was grappling with that, 'And right now I'm more interested in knowing who you are.' Instinctively Mornay went to leave her chair. She had forgotten, however, the swiftness with which he could move. In one moment her wrist was once more manacled, and he was looking tough when he said, as she sank back on to her chair, 'You've got about three minutes before Sister comes back in which to tell me who you are.' Stubbornly Mornay glared at him. 'If you don't tell me,' he ignored her angry look to continue bluntly, 'then you'll leave me no option but to tell her that you're the woman who knocked me down

and who—despite calls for the driver to come forward—
has declined to do so.'

'You don't know it was me!' she challenged hotly. 'You
can't verify anything,' she went rapidly on, not seeing
how, with her maroon-coloured car hidden in its garage,
anyone could make the assumption he had. Convinced
that he could prove none of his deductions, Mornay
warmed to her theme as she went on stoutly, 'Just because I happened to be on the scene last night when the
ambulance arrived to——'

'I could,' he sliced in crisply, 'let you go on. But you've
already hung yourself with your lies—any barrister I
employed would make mincemeat of you inside two
minutes,' he inserted. 'However...' As Mornay stared
at him, and as her blood ran cold at that word 'barrister', he suddenly closed his eyes. 'However,' he went
on a second later, 'I've something of a thundering
headache and I think Sister might have got it right when
she indicated I should be quiet. So, since I wasn't brought
to this establishment by ambulance but by——'

'You—weren't?' Mornay gasped, and saw his tired
eyes open.

'As luck would have it,' he told her, 'one of the first
people on the scene was a passing doctor heading this
way. He stopped—you didn't. I'll have your name,' he
stated, and looked so decidedly groggy that Mornay was
tempted to go looking for someone on the nursing staff.
'Your name,' he repeated.

'Mornay Haynes,' she told him, and, as he closed his
eyes and seemed to her to have lost colour he did not
have, she was awash with guilt that she'd exhausted him
more by not telling him her name sooner.

The hold on her wrist slackened and, looking down
on him, she saw that he had fallen asleep. Leaving the
flowers on his bedside locker, she moved silently to the
door. She had the door open when she realised that he
was not asleep as she had thought.

'Come and see me tomorrow,' he suddenly commanded.

Mornay turned swiftly. 'But . . .' she tried to protest, and then saw that she was wasting her breath. It didn't matter whether he was asleep or whether he wasn't. What he was, was used up. She was doing him no kindness by staying there to argue.

She left the side-ward just as the sister hove into view. Mornay bade her good afternoon, but she was overwhelmingly relieved when she saw her go into the side-ward to take a look at her patient.

Mornay was going out through the hospital gates when she surfaced from being stunned by all that had so recently happened, to recall that Mr Probert had specifically given her some time off so that she could go and visit her sister. Turning about, Mornay made her way back inside the hospital.

For once she felt no heart to go and see Claudia, but since Mr Probert was bound to ask how she was when he saw her she aimed her feet in the direction of the maternity wing. She did not want to lie to Mr Probert and, since it had been proved that she was so awful at it, she began to wish that she had never embarked on a course of untruths that day.

That was not all she wished. Heartily then did she wish that she had not given the man in the accident wing her correct name. Where her brain had been then she had no idea but, away from the man and the panic he had caused her, it seemed to her that she had been particularly stupid. If she was going to give him a name at all, for goodness' sake, why hadn't she thought to give him a false one?

Perhaps he'll forget it, she mused hopefully as she neared the double doors of the maternity wing. He'd looked exhausted, she recalled, as she pushed through the first set of doors, so perhaps her name had not properly registered with him.

Mornay was going through the second set of double doors when she tried to come to terms with his astounding announcement that he had not lost his memory. How she wished she had known that before. Had she known in advance that there was nothing wrong with his memory, then she was certain that never would she have been so soft-hearted as to put a foot inside the accident wing.

She sighed as she circumnavigated a large table in the middle of the maternity ward and headed for the far end, where she could see Claudia with her head stuck in a paperback. She didn't know who the dickens the man was, for she had been too shaken to ask him his name, but, while he might never have lost his memory as he'd stated, it was clear that he had no memory of the actual accident. For had he had any memory of her car heading straight for him, since he had seemed to her to be looking directly into her car, he might well have remembered that the driver—with his bushy beard—was male.

'Mornay! What a nice surprise!' Claudia lowered her book just as her sister reached the end of her bed. 'I didn't expect any visitors until this evening!'

'I'm sitting with the girls tonight, so Mr Probert kindly gave me some time off so I could visit you this afternoon. Now,' she said cheerfully, 'what's this I hear about your temperature?'

'Wouldn't you know it? Just when I'm bursting to get home to show my daughters their new brother, my temperature has to go into orbit.'

'You could,' Mornay suggested, 'make the most of it. With five children and a husband, you'll have your work cut out when you get home.'

'I know,' Claudia agreed, and then, serious for once, 'but I do so love my home.'

'I know you do,' Mornay said softly, knowing full well how determined her sister was that her home would always be a warm, joyous and secure place for her family, and not in any way like the cold and strict home she had left at the first opportunity.

'I couldn't bear for anything to happen that would spoil it,' Claudia told her quietly.

At that point Mornay realised that her sister, because of her enforced stay, was on the brink of subsiding into the doldrums. 'Then we'll have to take jolly good care that nothing does,' she teased brightly.

'Promise?' Claudia responded to her teasing with a smile.

'I promise,' Mornay told her, and she was the more serious of the two at that time.

Claudia was much on Mornay's mind when for the second time that afternoon she left the hospital. So too, was the other person she had 'inadvertently' visited. Claudia's security was paramount, but he had looked so dreadful. Oh, what a muddle it all was. And she was in the middle of it.

There was she, freely promising—and meaning that promise even if it was in joking fashion—that she would guard Claudia's security for her, while at the same time the one person who was the greatest threat to that security was demanding that she pay him a visit tomorrow.

Mornay had reached the Town Hall when, her mind in a turmoil, she caught sight of a paper-seller at his usual stand. In an attempt to pin her thoughts on other things, she went over and purchased a copy of an early edition of the evening paper. Mr Probert was an avid bargain-hunter and liked to scan the 'Going for a Song' ads.

Intending to give the paper to him as soon as she reached his office, Mornay was just ascending the Town Hall steps when, as she glanced to the paper in her hand, a banner headline on the front page caught her eye—and she stopped dead.

With her heart beating ten to the dozen she opened the paper out. 'Industrialist recovers memory', the headline read. Quickly Mornay read the rest of it. Apparently the victim of last evening's hit-and-run accident had been staying at the Belvedere, one of the two prestigious hotels in town. It had been an extremely warm evening and he had left his hotel dressed in shirt-sleeves and trousers and without identification on him. The recovery of his memory, so the paper said, had been prompted when the manager of the Belvedere had that morning heard the news on the radio, and had come forward to report that one of his guests was missing.

Mornay clearly remembered that the man she had seen that afternoon had plainly told her that he had never lost his memory to begin with. But that didn't concern her then, because there was something else she remembered. Not an hour ago she had thought how she did not know the man's name. At the end of reading the report that covered most of the front page, she knew quite well who he was—and wished that she didn't. For the man who had last night been pole-axed by a hit-and-run driver was none other than the wealthy components manufacturer, Bradford Kendrick. Brad Kendrick, so it was said, had come up the hard way and was an 'eye for an eye' type. No man, according to the report, ever put one over on him without living to regret it.

Oh, grief, Mornay thought, did that go for women too?

CHAPTER THREE

AFTER another restless night, Mornay got up the next morning word-perfect with the report she had read in yesterday's paper about Brad Kendrick, thirty-six, industrialist, bachelor, and at present a patient in Reefingham General. So she should be word-perfect, she mused glumly—she had read the report often enough.

She had taken the paper with her to show Gerry when she'd gone to babysit, but he'd already seen it. 'Don't worry,' he'd advised. 'Just sit tight—it'll soon blow over. Now I must get going, Claudia will be watching the ward doors. Be good, girls,' he had instructed his daughters.

There hadn't been time then to tell him about the idiot she had been that afternoon, and when he'd returned he'd been a bit quiet because there had seemed some doubt that Claudia would be coming home the next day either, and Mornay had thought better than to worry him with a blow-by-blow account of how crass she had been.

Thinking over everything that had happened as she got ready for work that Wednesday morning, Mornay sorely wished that she could turn the clock back to two days ago. If she had known then what she knew now, there was no way she would have allowed Gerry to drive her car. No way she would have gone celebrating with him—be it only one drink. And for certain, she would have avoided Reefingham's High Street like the plague.

Guilt was her companion once more when for the second morning running she opted to walk to work. The other headline in yesterday's paper concerned the bank raid; thankfully the police were busy with that and had not so far, made any headway with the 'hit and run'. Mornay was grateful for small mercies, but she was not of a mind to advertise the dent in her Metro by driving it around in broad daylight—she'd done a detour of the town to get to Penny Dale last night.

'Good morning, Mr Probert,' she greeted her boss with every sign that she had nothing more serious on her mind than what shade of lipstick to buy next. Then, remembering how she had barely earned her corn yesterday, she put all her efforts into having a better work day that day and for the first hour showed tremendous results.

Around ten o'clock, however, she discovered that her concentration was wavering. Too often she found she was having to pull her thoughts back from the fact that Brad Kendrick was expecting her to pay him a visit that afternoon.

As she had yesterday, she hoped he would forget her name. But, as the hour hand on the office clock crawled round, Mornay began to hope that he would have forgotten too that he had 'commanded' her, 'Come and see me tomorrow'.

Oh, lord, she worried, and began to fret that if he *had* remembered her name then—with him being an 'eye for an eye' merchant and everything—if she didn't visit him as ordered, all he had to do was to tell the police her name and they'd find her inside two minutes! Since her parents had left the area, the only person going by the name of 'Haynes' listed in the telephone book as living locally was her.

Mornay was starting to have horrifying visions of him having called the police anyway, and of the police being there at the hospital waiting for her if she did turn up that day, when Gerry rang.

'They're not ready to let Claudia home yet,' he told her. 'Can you do the honours and babysit again to-night? I sort of got the impression when I just rang my mother that it will be many a long day before she'll come and sit again.'

'Of course I'll come,' Mornay said at once, mentally ruling out the evening as a time when she might have obeyed Brad Kendrick's summons.

She returned to her desk after lunch with the word 'barrister' in her head, the threat it implied making her feel quite ill. An hour later she accepted from the jitteriness inside her that she was fooling only herself if she thought she wasn't going hospital visiting that afternoon. Brad Kendrick had the upper hand. She, by virtue of going into the accident wing yesterday, had given it to him.

'Any chance of my having an hour off?' she asked Mr Probert.

'Want to go and see your sister?' he asked understandingly.

'I'd like to go to the hospital,' she replied.

Which, she thought as her feet trod the same path they had yesterday, must rank among one of the biggest lies she had told to date. She would not like to go to the hospital. No way did she want to go to the hospital. But, because she was having to jump to Brad Kendrick's tune, Reefingham General—and the accident wing in particular—was where she was heading.

Her fears that the police might be waiting for her were proved unfounded. Not that she had given serious thought to that alarming possibility. The person who was waiting for her when she went through the first set of double doors of the accident wing, however, was the ward sister who had been on duty yesterday.

That was to say that the ward sister's office door was open and, as Mornay paused prior to plucking up her courage ready to go into the side-ward, the sister came out from behind her door.

'Mr Kendrick's been transferred to the private wing, and has left word that you must be his only visitor,' the sister told her, plainly remembering her from yesterday. 'Do you know where it is?'

'I think so, thank you,' Mornay smiled, but thanked Mr Kendrick not for the privilege he afforded her. She turned about and headed for the more recently added-on wing, and asked the next nursing sister she saw, 'May I see Mr Kendrick, please?'

'I'm afraid he's not seeing visitors,' she was informed.

'Oh,' Mornay said, and had half turned away when a worrying thought struck her. 'He's not worse, is he?' she asked, while at the same time the lady in charge was asking her name. 'The sister in the accident wing said he would see me,' Mornay replied, having foolishly revealed her name yesterday and not likely to make that mistake a second time.

'You're Miss . . .'

'Haynes,' Mornay supplied resignedly, and received a smile for her trouble and an apology for not being allowed in without question.

'The world and his wife have been trying to get in to see him today,' the neat, professional woman told her. 'He's just not up to giving Press interviews yet,' she went on as she escorted her down a short corridor, took a right turn and, with the words, 'You won't stay too long, will you?' departed.

From choice, Mornay would have preferred to have made this visit the shortest on record. But, taking a deep breath, she tapped softly on the door, and went in.

'You took your time!' the man propped up on pillows gritted aggressively.

Very much wishing that she had never come at all, Mornay went forward to the bed. By the sound of it, his ill-humour of yesterday had not improved any. 'How are you feeling today?' she enquired politely, and, realising that she had to make the best of it, she pulled a chair up to the bed and sat down.

'How do you think I feel?' he grunted. 'It's not every day that I get mown down by an armour-plated truck.'

Strangely, the fact that he could so exaggerate having been knocked over by her car brought a smile to her lips. 'Austin Metro, actually,' she said quite without thinking and, even as she was inwardly wincing at the easy way he had extracted that piece of information from her, she was receiving yet another sharp edge of his tongue.

'I'm glad you find it amusing!' he bit out, his dark glance fixing on the upward curve of her attractive mouth.

Instantly Mornay straightened her expression. 'I don't find it a bit amusing,' she told him coolly. 'It was just that with you saying——' She broke off, irritated by him. How could she explain to this bad-tempered brute that something in his exaggerated comment had triggered her sense of humour? 'Are you in pain?' she changed course to enquire, thinking that the pain he might be enduring was responsible for his acerbic attitude—he looked more rested than yesterday but didn't have very much more colour.

'Had you been drinking?' he ignored her question to ask one of his own.

'I'd been celebr——' Abruptly she halted, wondering what it was about this man that had her speaking without first engaging her brain.

'You'd been celebrating!' he quickly caught on to what she had just bit back. 'You were *drunk*!' he accused harshly.

'No, I *wasn't*!' she denied vehemently. 'I had only one drink to——' Again she broke off.

'What were you celebrating?' he demanded to know.

'That's none of your business!' she rapped back smartly for his nerve, and ignored the narrowing of his eyes that spoke of him not caring very much for her tone. She was unrepentant though—she had already, unwarily, revealed more than she had intended, and had

no intention of telling him anything that might lead him
to speculate on anything connected with her sister—or
her sister's family.

'I could,' he threatened silkily, 'make it my business.'

Oh, dear heaven, Mornay panicked, and as that word
'barrister' popped up in her brain again, she was back-
pedalling fast. 'Er—there was quite a write-up on you
in the local paper yesterday, Mr Kendrick,' she pulled
out of a panicky nowhere, hoping to distract him.

'But nothing about you, I take it,' he drawled.

Mornay, who up until then had never known an
emotion as fierce as hate, suddenly felt that she hated
Bradford Kendrick. 'I'd hardly be likely to be here now
if there had been!' she snapped, and didn't care a bit
when she saw it register that, but for his blackmailing
her to come and visit him that afternoon, she would have
found something of a pleasanter nature to do.

He did not make further comment on it, however, but,
with a rapidly fired question that was at variance with
the still debilitated look of him, he abruptly asked,
'Where do you live?'

'In Reefingham,' she replied, knowing for sure that
he could find that much out for himself without much
help now that he knew her name.

'Where?' he further shot at her.

Mornay was getting a little fed up with him and, as
stubbornness paid her a visit, she felt she'd be hanged
if she'd volunteer her address.

'In a flat,' she replied coldly.

'With your family?' was his next cannon shot—and
Mornay sensed danger. She felt then that he must not
by any means know that she had a sister.

'My parents live in Solihull,' she told him, and wished
that she hadn't—but it was too late then. 'You live in
London, I belive,' she said in a desperate bid to get him
off a subject that was too close for comfort. 'According
to yesterday's early evening edition, you live——'

'For the moment, I live here!' he cut in in disgruntled fashion. 'Though not for much longer,' he added inflexibly.

From hating him Mornay swung to being afraid for him. 'Surely they're not thinking of letting you go?' she questioned, thinking it only natural that she should feel some disquiet, for he still looked far from well.

'They,' he retorted, 'have no option.'

'No option?' she queried, staring at him, at his firm chin, and even as she queried his remark she realised that it would be a brave man who tried to oppose him once he had made up his mind to anything.

'I've had it with this enforced incarceration,' Brad Kendrick told her in no uncertain terms, and caused Mornay to stare at him some more when he announced, 'I'm leaving tomorrow.'

Mornay had never received any medical training, but felt then that she needed none to know that he would be better for staying in bed for a week. In her view, even a person with limited vision would be able to see that by no chance was Brad Kendrick ready to leave hospital tomorrow.

'You can't!' she told him bluntly, and saw his right eyebrow shoot aloft at what he clearly thought her sauce.

'Watch me!' he mocked.

'But—you're not well! You need someone to look after you,' she tried to get him to see reason, forgetful when looking at the enervated state of him that she should be rejoicing that he was talking of leaving Reefingham and going back to London. Yet, suddenly, when she saw that a thinking look had come to him, she was beginning to doubt the evidence of her eyes. Something, she realised, had just occurred to him, and had given him an alert look. 'You have someone in your London home who'll look after you?' she enquired, wondering, since he was reported as unmarried, if he'd remembered he had a relation or a housekeeper who would look after him.

But no, he was shaking his head, and suddenly Mornay did not like at all the pleasant expression with which he masked his inner thoughts. Nor did she like in the least the solution which had just come to him when, his words more silky than pleasant, he softly drawled, 'Since you're responsible for the position I'm in, Miss Haynes, I'll— let you do it.'

'What?' she questioned, aghast, quite certain just then that her normally quite bright brain was having a day off and that she must be misunderstanding what it sounded as though he was telling her.

'I'll let you look after me,' he elucidated evenly. 'I'm sure——'

But, realising that she had not misunderstood him at all, Mornay wasted not a moment to cut him off. 'I'm not going to London with you!' she erupted hotly. 'You——' She was cut off this time.

'I never asked you to,' he told her forthrightly.

'But—but . . .' she stammered, and did not care for the phoney smile he bestowed on her.

'I'll come to your flat,' he announced, and while she stared, incredulous and disbelieving, 'A month's convalescence is the minimum you owe me,' he stated in a tone there was no arguing with.

But Mornay did argue. Convalescence! A month! A month with him in her tiny flat! 'That's impossible!' she told him shortly—and that was before she thought of the other complications.

Abruptly any sign of a smile, phoney or otherwise, left him. 'You have a ''live-in'' lover?' he demanded furiously, all too clearly a man who did not like to have his plans thwarted.

'No!' she flared, before she could think, and saw his anger fade.

'In that case you can come and collect me at ten tomorrow morning.' He had it instantly all worked out.

'But I can't,' she tried to get through to him. 'I've only one bedroom and——'

'Set your mind at rest, Miss Haynes. I——' he clipped '—shall not want to share it,' and for the first time in her life Mornay experienced an almost uncontrollable urge to hit someone. She was sure that she was more than gratified at this vitriolic man's point-blank assertion that he didn't fancy her, but that didn't stop her from wanting to box his ears just the same. She came even closer to wanting to set about him when, toughly, he added, 'Take my word for it, one more night here is all I'm putting up with.'

'But . . .' she tried to protest.

'Ten tomorrow morning,' he stated coldly, his blunt tone telling her that she would be wasting her breath in trying to get him to change his mind.

Mornay thought she might have had another try just the same, had the ward sister not chosen just that exact moment to enter the room, and with a smile to Mornay she came to take a closer look at her patient. 'You've got a bad head again, haven't you?' she declared. Mornay, taking the hint that in Sister's view she had overstayed her welcome, returned her chair to the spot from where she had collected it, and left.

Her mind was in such a ferment, though, that she was back at her office and Mr Probert was asking, 'How was your sister?' before she realised that she hadn't given Claudia a thought.

'About the same,' she replied and, not wanting to lie to him, she avoided any more questions by getting down straight away to some work.

The work she had chosen to tackle, though, was matter which did not require one hundred per cent concentration, and in no time Mornay was going over the same thoughts that had gone through her mind on the way back from the hospital. Despite Brad Kendrick's *deciding* to lodge himself in her flat for a month, it was

just impossible. For so much as a week it was impossible—oh, what on earth was she going to do?

Aside from the fact of her flat having only one
bedroom, the rest of it, with its sitting-room that did
service as a dining-room too, and its poky kitchen and
equally poky bathroom, was barely big enough for her—
and he, though without spare flesh, was a big man.

Mornay had done nothing about asking Mr Probert
for some time off the following morning when at five
o'clock that evening he stopped by her desk and asked,
'Haven't you a home to go home to?'

'I'll just finish this,' she said knowing that she
wouldn't be able to work too late if she were to be at
Penny Dale for a quarter to seven. 'I . . .' she began, but
because she did not honestly and truly want the time off
she had to invent something else to say when he halted
expectantly. 'It won't take me long,' she smiled.

When half an hour later she left her office, she knew
full well that it just wasn't on for Brad Kendrick to stay
with her for a month. She didn't have the first clue about
nursing anyway—and somebody was going to have to
keep an eye on him in the early days of his leaving the
hospital.

She let herself into her flat, having time only for a
quick cup of tea, and pondered that, just supposing that
her flat were big enough to share with that six-foot-plus
broad-shouldered individual, then—what about the other
complications that would ensue? On an average of once
a week Claudia would ring up for a half-hour chat—
those chats had begun when she had first moved into
the flat and Claudia had feared that she might be lonely.
Mornay saw that she stood no chance of keeping from
'her lodger' the knowledge that she had a sister. Especially since it was not unknown for Claudia *and* Gerry
and the children to call in at some time over any given
weekend.

Shrugging aside the fact that Robert Naylor would be back from Wales on Friday if not before, and could well prove to be another complication, Mornay drove over to Penny Dale, racking her brains to think up some good reason for not presenting herself at the hospital in the morning to pick up Bradford Kendrick.

She reached her brother-in-law's home knowing the uselessness of hoping that the hospital would refuse to let him out. Even without what she had read about the wretched man and his determination in business, her instinct from what she personally knew of him so far told her that the hospital would not have a hope of holding him if he was determined to sign himself out.

'Everything OK with you?' Gerry queried, leaving the lawn where he had been watching his daughters playing on the swing he had put up, and coming to open the gate for her. 'You're looking a bit pale,' he commented.

That she looked a mite pale was no surprise to Mornay; she had barely slept since the accident, and what with one thing and another it was no wonder, she felt, that the strain should be showing. She felt near then to telling him what an idiot she had been yesterday and how, for her sins, she looked like having to put up with an unwanted convalescent for a month—starting to-morrow—unless she could think up something brilliant.

But, looking at Gerry, she could see that he didn't look as though he had slept much since the accident either, so, 'I'm fine,' she told him, and shooed him off to the hospital realising that, for all he wasn't outwardly showing it, he must be concerned to know how far he could trust her to stay quiet. On top of that, Mornay knew that he would not be truly happy until Claudia was back home.

'Are you going to read to us, Mornay?' Emily, who chose to do away with the title 'aunt', broke into Mornay's thoughts.

'What a good idea,' Mornay congratulated her, and, thinking to have the four girls bathed and in bed by the time Gerry returned, 'Have you had supper?' she asked.

'Daddy gave us ''ghetti bol'naise'',' three-year-old Prudence attempted.

'And told us not to tell Mummy that it came out of a tin,' Alice confided.

'I'll bet it was lovely,' Mornay murmured, and did not have another moment in which to think her own thoughts until an hour and a half later when Gerry returned. While he went upstairs to spend ten minutes with his wide-awake daughters, she went downstairs to make a cup of coffee.

Having decided against asking him how Claudia was in front of his daughters in case the sound of her name brought forth cries of 'I want Mummy', Mornay looked at him with the ready question on her lips when Gerry joined her.

'Terrific!' he told her before she could say a word. 'Claudia—with Luke, of course—is coming out of hospital tomorrow!'

'Oh, super!' Mornay exclaimed, and poured him a cup of coffee while he went into raptures about having Claudia back home and said how rudderless he had felt without her in the home.

Once coffee was out of the way he was then voicing the opinion that he'd better have a blitz round the place before the morning. 'You don't mind if I get the vacuum out, do you?' he asked.

Mornay enjoyed being a part of this family. 'Is that a basket of ironing I see?' she queried.

'Would you?' Gerry asked.

Mornay stayed in the kitchen and tackled the vast mountain of ironing while her brother-in-law went and cleaned the sitting-room. All too soon, though, her pleasing thoughts of her sister and her contented family unit started to get away from her, and into her head came the problem that had been with her since her own hospital visit that afternoon. What good reason could she find for not going to pick up Brad Kendrick in the morning?

She finished the last of the ironing having thought on the question for two solid hours. But, the best answer that had come to her was the answer she had already given—that there was no room in her flat for a guest—either wanted or, as in his case—unwanted.

She recalled how totally unimpressed he had been by her protestations that it was impossible for him to stay with her. 'Take my word for it,' he'd said, 'one more night here is all I'm putting up with.' Mornay unplugged the iron, and, deeply involved with her thoughts, she sighed, and did not hear her brother-in-law come in.

Only a few moments later did she realise that her expression must have revealed a lot of her inner tumult over the predicament she was in when he attracted her attention and looked at her worriedly. 'Mornay,' he said, 'you wouldn't do anything to destroy things for us, would you?'

From somewhere she found a smile, 'Rest easy, Gerry,' she told him.

A black cloud had descended on her thoughts as she drove herself home. Rest easy, she had told him—she wished that *she* could. The words 'One more night here is all I'm putting up with' were haunting her as she garaged her car and entered her apartment building.

She climbed the stairs to the first-floor landing, thinking disheartenedly that, if one counted baby Luke, then that was three people she knew who were coming out of hospital tomorrow—if she couldn't think up a way of ensuring that one of them stayed put. Petrifying visions then began to penetrate of her leaving the hospital with her unwanted guest tomorrow and coming face to face with Claudia and Gerry. It wouldn't take Gerry long to calculate who the stranger was by her side. Her brother-in-law would have a heart attack on the spot, she thought agitatedly.

But it wasn't going to come to that. Somehow, she must find a way of getting out of going to the hospital in the morning—but how? Oh, dear heaven, she began to panic as she made to turn the corner of the landing where she had her flat. If she wasn't at the hospital at ten to pick up Brad Kendrick in the morning then she didn't give much for her chances of not hearing from the police shortly afterwards. Oh, grief, Gerry... Abruptly, her thoughts stopped—frozen in shock!

No, her brain tried to deny what her eyes were telling her as she halted, horrified, in her tracks. Her thoughts then became rapidly chaotic, because evidence that there would be only two people to her knowledge leaving the hospital—not three—was there before her very eyes! Witness to the fact that one male of the species, with whom she was desperately wishing she had never come into contact, could not put up with even just 'one more night' in hospital was there in front of her.

'Oh, no!' she cried huskily, but, no matter how much she might want to protest, there was no getting away from it. All the proof she needed that she would not now be required to present herself at the private wing of Reefingham General tomorrow was there in the sound-asleep man who, with his long legs stretched out before him, was propped up against her flat door. Bradford Kendrick—with an expensive-looking overnight case by his side—had already left hospital!

CHAPTER FOUR

WONDERING how long he'd been there asleep on the landing outside her flat—for surely the hospital would have tried to dissuade him from leaving any later than eight, and it was going on for eleven now—Mornay realised that she just couldn't leave him there and, as was tempting, tiptoe away.

'Mr Kendrick!' she bent down to whisper his name, fearing to disturb the other residents, while quietly thinking that the gods must really have been kind if he'd been propped up outside her flat for a couple of hours and no one had seen him. 'Mr Kendrick!' she repeated, a little louder this time when he slept on. 'Brad!' she used his first name in an endeavour to get through to him when he slept on.

Abruptly his eyes opened and she found herself looking directly into a pair of intelligent dark eyes. 'What?' he asked.

'You can't sleep here,' she told him.

'I'm not returning to hospital,' he told her in that forthright way she was getting to know.

'I didn't mean that,' she told him and, observing that he was looking quite ill, 'Come on,' she told him more kindly, 'you'd better come in.'

'That sounds like a good idea,' he responded, but seemed so determined not to flinch as she stood back and he got to his feet that she felt certain that he must ache in every bone in his body.

She was convinced of it when, his face totally lacking in colour, he leant against the door-frame while she quickly found her key and unlocked the door. Somehow, though, when she experienced an urge to take a hold of his arm and help him into her apartment, she managed to resist it. One way or another, she instinctively felt that he would take exception to any such show of evidence that she was aware of his physical vulnerability.

'This way,' she told him, and did the next best thing, which was to pick up his overnight case and, leaving him to follow, carry it for him into her neat and tidy and pleasantly furnished, if small, sitting-cum-dining-room. 'Where did this come from, by the way?' she enquired as, holding out his case, she turned and saw that he had secured the door behind him.

'I had the hotel pack my few belongings and bring them to the hospital,' he muttered, and looked so rocky that Mornay thought that he actually swayed on his feet.

'You'd better sit down,' she told him, and whether he liked it or not she placed his case to the floor and went over to guide him to her two-seater couch.

She wasn't sure that a grateful grunt did not leave him as the couch took his weight, but he had his eyes closed and as she looked at him she wondered what the blazes she did with him now. He had said categorically that he wasn't returning to the hospital, and, since he'd got the hotel he'd previously been staying in to send over his belongings, she reckoned that she didn't need to ask how he felt about going to a hotel for the night.

As she looked at him, though, she was suddenly again smitten by guilt. He looked terrible and she felt partly to blame—how in creation could she think of sending him anywhere, the condition he was in?

Mornay stayed looking at him for only long enough to observe that, exhausted, he seemed to have fallen asleep again, and then she went quietly and quickly to her airing cupboard. A very short while later she had her bed stripped and remade with clean linen and had taken his case in her bedroom. She then returned to the man who was still sitting on her couch with his eyes closed.

'Mr Kendrick,' she awakened him gently.

'What happened to "Brad"?' he enquired as his eyes came open, showing that, if his body was temporarily broken, his brain was as alert as ever.

'When did you last eat?' she asked him.

'I'm not hungry.'

'Would you like anything to drink?' He shook his head and, catching his involuntary wince, Mornay knew that his head was bad. 'Did the hospital give you any medication?' she asked.

'In my case,' he replied.

'It's time you were in bed,' she told him, and had confirmation that he was done in when, not giving her the smallest argument, he left the couch.

With stiff movements he followed her to the bedroom. If he had any colour then as he sat down on her bed, it was grey. Oh, the poor man, Mornay thought, and was past caring then that by no means did she want him inside her flat.

'The sooner you're in bed, the sooner you'll start to feel better,' she told him, and began to help him out of his lightweight jacket.

'I'll take your word for it,' he mumbled as, used up, it seemed, he allowed her to unfasten the buttons of his shirt.

Mornay left him while he removed his shirt and went to his case and unfastened it. There was a phial of tablets on top which she removed and went to place on the bedside table. Then she returned to his case to hunt for his nightwear. 'They've forgotten your pyjamas,' she told him when her search proved fruitless.

'I don't use them,' he replied, and for no reason she could think of Mornay felt her cheeks go pink.

'Oh,' she mumbled and, unaware that his eyes had followed her and that he had been watching her, she got

herself together, realising that there was more to this
nursing of the wounded than she had bargained for.

Avoiding looking at his face, or his broad bare chest,
she knew that, just as there was no way he was going to
spend a comfortable night dressed as he was, there was
also no way he was going to find the energy to shed his
trousers without her help.

Attempting to appear matter-of-fact, she returned to
the man sitting on the edge of her bed and extended a
shaky hand to the waistband of his trousers. Though
suddenly, with a quickness she had experienced before,
he snaked out a hand to her wrist and was putting her
hand away from his person. And when at the same time,
'Well, I'll be . . .' hit her ears, all the sensitive empathy
she had for the way he must be feeling abruptly vanished
as Brad Kendrick followed it up with, 'As I live and
breathe—you're a virgin!'

Realising that there must have been something tell-
tale about her actions, she snapped, 'What's that got to
do with anything?'

'Don't be cross with me, Mornay,' he smiled, 'my head
won't stand it.'

'Oh, I'm sorry,' she said, instantly contrite.

'Why don't you go and fetch me a drink of water?'
he suggested tiredly, and as she grabbed at his suggestion
and turned about he added, 'Let the tap run for five
minutes.'

Seven minutes later Mornay returned to the bedroom
to see that Brad Kendrick, his trousers on the floor, was
in between the covers, and was once more asleep. As she
looked at his pale but relaxed face, compassion stabbed
at her and she watched him for some seconds, worried
if she should wake him to see that he took his medication. Though maybe he had taken it while she had
been in the kitchen. She watched him for a minute or
so, then it suddenly seemed to her that, even without his
tablets, to sleep soundly might do him as much good.

Quietly she placed the glass of water she had brought upon the bedside table in case he awakened thirsty in the night. Then she picked up his trousers and hung them tidily over the back of a chair, together with the rest of his clothes. Then, collecting her night things, she switched out the light and, leaving the door very slightly ajar so that she should hear him should he be in some distress during the night, she quietly left the room.

Her settee, Mornay discovered within a very short space of time, had never been designed with the comforts of sleep in mind. She tried sleeping on her back, then on her right side and then on her left, and a couple of hours later she estimated that if she'd managed to sleep for ten minutes, that was the sum total.

Think pleasant thoughts, she instructed herself, but within seconds her thinking was again centred on Brad Kendrick. The poor man had been worn out, she reflected, and guessed that he had used up what reserves of energy he had left by getting to her flat. The stairs up to the first floor must have seemed like a mountain!

Another two hours of totalling only another ten minutes of sleep, and Mornay's sensitive thoughts on the convalescent next door had undergone something of a change. Why did he have to come and park himself on her—he knew that he wasn't welcome!

Another tortuous hour went by and Mornay knew that somehow she was going to get him out of her flat. He'd stated quite unequivocally that a month's convalescence was the minimum she owed him, but she was beginning to feel that she'd be a nervous wreck before the end of one week, let alone four.

Dawn had broken when from pure fatigue Mornay at last got to sleep for longer than ten minutes. With Brad Kendrick forever on her mind, though, her last conscious and agitated memory was of reading that no man ever put one over on him without living to regret it.

She awakened a couple of hours later and found that her thoughts were instantly on the same treadmill. Anyone might call or phone and cause a slip which would alert that highly intelligent man who was now hogging her bed to the fact that she was not the driver who knocked him down. Somehow, she just had to get him out of her flat.

Knowing for sure that she was not going to sleep any more, Mornay moved the bedspread which had covered her during the night and, dressing-gown-clad, she went quietly to take a look at her 'guest'.

Having earned herself a few stiff joints from the awkwardness of cramping her fairly tall self on to her fairly short couch, she had some small inkling of the 'all over' ache Brad Kendrick must be enduring as she tiptoed into the bedroom.

He was asleep still, she saw, and as a wave of compassion once more smote her she wished with all she had that the accident had never happened. With warm, gentle eyes she stared at his high forehead, his straight nose, and his firm chin and, crazily, she suddenly felt the most absurd impulse to rest a hand on his forehead. Somehow she felt that by stroking his forehead she might stroke away any after-effects from the accident that he was still suffering.

A moment later she was never more glad that she had not given heed to that impulse, for abruptly his eyes opened and he was awake. Strangely then—when if she had expected anything it would have been for him to straight away be his usual acerbic self—to her surprise he smiled! She saw his glance go from her eyes, to take in her make-up-free unblemished skin and to her sleep-tousled blonde hair, and still he smiled. It was a slow smile, a gentle smile and, she was certain, genuine.

Feeling most peculiarly affected from seeing a first genuine smile on him, Mornay found her mouth curving upwards, and she was able to do no other than smile back. 'Good morning,' she bade him quietly, and then, realising that she must be smiling at him like an idiot, she turned swiftly about and was going through the doorway when she threw over her shoulder, 'I'll just go and get bathed and dressed.'

It did not take Mornay long, when in her bathroom she tried a spot of self-analysis, to realise that what had come over her a minute or two ago had been nothing more alarming than shyness. She was unused to having a male guest spending the night in her flat. In fact she had never had a male overnight guest in her flat, so it was hardly to be wondered at that she should feel a little peculiar about it—a little shy.

Pleased with her diagnosis, Mornay was quicker than usual in her bath that morning and was soon dressed in a summer dress suitable for the office, and had the tousled look brushed from her long hair.

For no known reason she took a deep breath and squared her shoulders before she went to take another peek at her 'guest'. To her consternation, however, he was not in the bedroom where she fully expected him to be, but, up and dressed, he was in her sitting-room.

'You shouldn't be out of bed!' she exclaimed in concern, seeing for herself how stiff his movements were when he came away from taking a look out of the window.

There was not so much as a glimmer of a smile about him now, she observed when, clearly taking exception to any idea she might have of bossing him around, 'I've had enough of bed,' he told her forthrightly, in 'end of subject' tones.

There was not a smile about Mornay either as, starting to get more than a degree fed up, and with thoughts of Claudia and how if she didn't go over to see her and the new baby tonight she reckoned she could be sure Claudia would be on the phone, she grew as forthright as him.

'If you're that well,' she snapped, as a hundred and one complications of his being there piled in, 'you're well enough to go home!'

If she was blunt, however, Brad Kendrick was blunter. 'I'm staying here!' he snarled, his chin jutting as though to say, argue with that.

'You can't!' Mornay tried.

'Why?' Ice was starting to glitter in his eyes as he challenged her to give him some good reason.

'Because...' she began hotly, and stopped. 'Because...' she attempted again, 'because I have to go to work, that's why!'

'You have a job—looking after me!' he informed her sharply, but as again Mornay felt the urge to physically lash out at him she saw the way he involuntarily rubbed a hand across his brow and, for all they were not quite yelling at each other, she realised that he was just not up to a shouting match.

Without another word she walked past him and into the kitchen. It was from there that she heard the bathroom door close, and she got on with the job of making a pot of tea and rummaging in her cupboards for something with which to feed the brute. She knew little about nursing, but it seemed to her that if he was to take his medication it would be best to have some foundation put down first.

She was in the dining-room part of the sitting-room, laying the table, when, showered and clean-shaven, Bradford Kendrick came from the bathroom and into the room.

'If you'd like to sit here, Mr Kendrick, I'll get you some scrambled eggs on toast,' she said, indicating one of the dining chairs, her tone even as she observed that just the action of shaving and showering seemed to have taken the stuffing out of him.

She turned away as he drew near to the table, and was on her way back to the kitchen when she heard him drawl, 'You can't call me Mr Kendrick for a month—make it Brad.'

Any kind feelings which might have surfaced were quickly banished as, thanking him not for his unsubtle hint, she was more concerned with getting him out of her apartment than putting up with him for a month. She glanced at her watch as she stirred eggs in the saucepan and knew that she didn't stand a hope of getting to her office on time.

But, 'Here we are!' she exclaimed breezily as she carried a tray containing both their breakfasts into the dining area. He did not seem at all impressed by her attempt to put a brave face on matters, though, and as she took her place opposite him she began to wonder if he was always such a bundle of joy or—was he in pain? 'You must take your tablets after breakfast,' she began as he picked up his knife and fork.

'I already did,' he grunted.

'Do you have a headache?' she queried kindly, and got a sour look for her trouble. Clearly Brad Kendrick was not the sort to down medication unless *he* considered it absolutely essential.

Silence reigned over the table as she set her mind to think up some tactful way to get him to leave without drawing his obstinate streak. She looked to his face, saw that he now seemed to have a trace of colour, and, cheered by that, she was about to launch into her tactful 'please go home' plea, when she suddenly became aware of how ham-fistedly he was cutting up his toast.

Then it was that she noticed the bruising on his left wrist and realised that he must have instinctively put out his hands to protect himself when her Metro had come at him—his left hand coming off worse than his right.

She was well and truly conscious-stricken when, 'To hell with it!' he suddenly grunted and, tipping the scrambled egg off the toast, he forked the egg up using his right hand, and downed toast which he held in his left.

'Where there's a will...' Mornay smiled, and when he glanced disagreeably across the table at her she asked, 'Have you damaged your wrists very badly?'

'According to the hospital they'll be as good as new within a few more days,' he condescended to answer.

'How about the rest of you?' she enquired, and realised when his reply came that he had not taken her question at face-value.

'Whatever,' he shrugged, 'I've still decided to take a month off work.'

Biting back the snappy retort of 'I hope it keeps fine for you', Mornay chewed on the toast and marmalade and sought afresh for some tactful way to tell him to be gone without his astute brain seeing right through her.

She soon realised, though, from the way he had looked beneath the surface of her question, 'How about the rest of you?', that she was wasting her time using tact. John Blunt here would see straight through her 'tactfulness' in two seconds flat!

He had finished his scrambled eggs and toast and was partaking of tea when, still the same needing a gentle way in, Mornay suddenly found it in a polite-sounding, 'I never thought, Mr—er—Brad—would you have preferred coffee?'

'Tea's fine,' he grunted.

'Good,' she smiled, and then embarked on a hurried and speedily put together suggestion. 'I've been thinking that if you'd like to go to a hotel—let me finish——' she inserted quickly when it looked as though he might chop her off '—I'd drive you there, of course,' she added, and weathered his look of acid, to go charging on, 'Then I could come and see you after I've finished work and...' He was shaking his head well before she had come to the end, and, suddenly infuriated by him, she erupted stormily, 'Well, you can't stay here!'

Furiously she glared at him. Mildly, his glance taking in her sparking blue eyes, he stared back. Then, pleasantly, she heard again the question which she was beginning to believe he had been born asking. 'Why?' he queried.

'Because,' she began hotly, when just then her glance rested on the couch, 'because I'm *not* spending another night on *that*!' she told him forcefully.

'For a virgin,' he drawled mockingly, 'you're rather forward.'

'What does that mean?' Mornay flared. Somehow it had never occurred to her, with the giant-sized headache he'd had last night, that he would remember, let alone refer to, his pronouncement that she was a virgin.

'Weren't you saying that you preferred to bed in with me rather than spend another night——'

'I was not!' she hissed before he could finish, and it was no wonder to her then that she should so often feel like thumping him. He was the giddy limit—and that was without the wicked gleam that had just joined the mockery in his eyes.

'My apologies,' he offered insincerely, and, after some moments of appearing to be thinking seriously, 'I have it,' he murmured, and, looking straight into her wary blue eyes, he announced, 'We must—both—move out.'

'Both!' she exclaimed, not crediting her hearing.

But there was nothing wrong with her hearing, Brad Kendrick soon made that plain when he reminded her, 'You said yourself that I need someone to look after me,' and added, 'Now, where would you like to go?'

She was asleep. She must be dreaming this, Mornay tried to tell herself—though nightmare seemed a more accurate description. But it did not work. For one thing, she had her eyes open. For another she was looking straight into a pair of dark eyes—the eyes of a monster who was waiting—seriously—for her answer.

Though, even as she said, 'Scotland,' the furthest away spot she could think of, she just could not believe that he was as serious as he seemed with his statement that they should both move out.

'Anywhere in particular?' he enquired, and while as it started to get through to her that he jolly well was serious—deadly serious for all his former mockery—all she could do was dumbly shake her head.

She was still in a state of dazed shock when, her non-preference for a choice of destination in Scotland noted by him, she saw him flick a glance to his watch. As if he was now in charge of her, Mornay copied him. Her watch said five past nine, but she was feeling so shaken that it passed her by that she was already five minutes late for her office.

'Where's your phone?' was the next question Brad Kendrick asked, and Mornay started to come away from being shaken to note that he hadn't asked, 'Have you got a phone?' which seemed to confirm for her that he had found her address from the telephone book.

'It's plugged in in the kitchen at the moment,' she answered him, and sat staring after him when—his movements stiff—he left the table and headed for the kitchen.

From her seat at the dining table she heard sounds indicating that he was about to make contact with the outside world. Then, before she could start to panic that he might be ringing the police to identify her as the culprit who had knocked him over and who had driven on without stopping, she heard his voice, all authority, stating, 'Miss Boulter, please.' Then, 'Helen,' she heard him say, then a small pause when 'Helen' clearly recognised his voice and, obviously having been contacted by him previously, probably from the private ward, must have been asking how he was. 'I'm out of hospital now,' he told her and was then instructing, 'I'm having some time off—find me a hideaway in Scotland.' And while

Mornay, unashamedly eavesdropping, started to realise that maybe because he was so well known in the business world it was no wonder that he liked his privacy outside of it, hence his request for a 'hideaway', he was ending, obviously reading the digits of the telephone dial, 'Ring me back on this number.' And while Mornay realised too that 'Helen' must be his secretary, he gave her the number and promptly rang off.

And still Mornay could hardly believe it. 'Do you—*really*—intend to go to Scotland?' she just had to ask when he came back and retook his seat at the table.

'And that you should come with me,' he replied calmly and—obviously quite at home—helped himself to a slice of toast from the toast rack. 'So kind of you to offer to drive,' he murmured.

Mornay gave him a killing look, hoped his toast choked him and left the table to storm to the kitchen—where she began to tidy up. The man was a swine, she fumed as, not wanting him in her kitchen again, she unplugged the phone and went and plugged it into a socket in the sitting-room.

Without a word to him she cleared some of the used dishes from off the table and felt defeated when, catching a glimpse of the bruising on his left wrist, she realised that it would take some days before he was fit to drive himself anywhere.

Feeling, however, that she had not a thing that she wanted to say to him, she did some washing up and returned for the rest of the dishes to find that he had moved and was now resting on the settee.

She went back to the kitchen, torn between a desire to tell him to go and rest on the bed, and a desire to tell him to clear off. She busied herself with sudsy water, but was soon finished with her chores.

She felt disinclined to spend more time with him than she had to, however, and when she left the kitchen she went through to the bathroom to clean a bath that was already clean, and to generally give it a spruce-up.

It crossed her mind at one point to wonder what Brad Kendrick would do if she told him that it had been her brother-in-law who had been driving that night, and not her. But that notion did not linger for long. Hadn't the paper described Brad Kendrick as an 'eye for an eye' man? Wasn't he proving that now by insisting that in return for her injuring him she should pay by looking after him?

Whichever way she looked at it, it seemed to Mornay then that she had no option but to do everything that the wretched man said, because he'd find some other way of making Gerry pay—the obvious way: that of reporting him to the police.

Mornay was not at all certain why Brad Kendrick had not reported *her* to the police, anyway. But what she did know for certain was that somebody was going to be made to pay. Glumly she faced the fact that, if she did confess Gerry's part in the accident, when it came to the bottom line, it would be Claudia and her children who would ultimately suffer.

Mornay left the bathroom with a heavy heart—she had to go along with that monster—even if it meant going as far as Scotland. She was crossing the sitting-room and, she owned, not in the best frame of mind when, his voice light, Brad Kendrick halted her.

'Did you really sleep on this couch?' he enquired, having endured enough of it, it seemed, to be able to ascertain that its potential for ensuring a night of unbroken sleep was little short of murderous.

'Occasionally,' Mornay replied acidly, and would have gone on to the bedroom to tidy round when suddenly she was arrested by his laugh. She saw his face light up, felt a most peculiar sensation in her heart region, and realised, not only that her dry humour had amused him, but also that she must have eaten her toast too quickly.

Suddenly, however, her mind went a blank, and as his amusement faded she discovered that she was still standing in front of him, and that she was having to search really hard for something to say that would explain why she was still standing there looking at him.

'Er—what did the hospital say?' she pulled out of thin air.

'Say?' he enquired.

'When you told them you were leaving,' she enlightened him as she got herself together.

'What could they say?' he queried, and seemed so genuinely surprised by her question that she realised Brad Kendrick was a law unto himself. Quite plainly, when he decided to do something, he simply did not deign to consider that there might be any opposition.

Which, Mornay began to think a moment later, pretty well summed up what was happening with her. He had decided that, since she was responsible for his being incapacitated, she could jolly well look after him. When she, meaning a hotel locally, had hinted that she could look after him elsewhere, he, brooking no opposition, had gone to work on the idea.

'You said that your wrists will be as good as new within a few days,' she reminded him. 'What about the rest of you?' she enquired, wanting more of an answer to that than the one he'd given her before: that he'd taken a month off work.

'What about the rest of me?' he tossed her own question back at her, being deliberately obtuse, she felt sure.

Mornay gave him a look of hearty dislike—which bounced straight off him—and asked, 'Is it going to take long for you to recover completely?'

'No,' he replied promptly, but any joy Mornay found from that answer was negated when he added silkily, 'Especially with you right there to ensure that I rest.'

Gritting her teeth, Mornay ignored the first part of what he said and questioned him about the last part. 'Is that what they've said—that you have to rest?'

His reply was to give her a cool look. But, even though he seemed to have grown bored with discussing his health and had now clammed up, Mornay felt she could be fairly certain that to rest was the instruction his doctor had given him on leaving the hospital.

Since Brad Kendrick seemed to have nothing more he wanted to say, Mornay left him and spent some time tidying the bedroom—which was tidy to start with. She really ought to ring Mr Probert, she thought worriedly, though she supposed she was still hoping against hope that she might be putting in some time at her office that day. She next thought that maybe a phone call to her brother-in-law dropping a hint of what was happening might not be a bad idea. Though how she could ring Gerry with her 'guest' sitting so close to the telephone she'd no idea. Gerry would only panic anyway, if she did ring him, she decided, and forgot the idea totally when she realised that, since Gerry would not delay in going to fetch her sister home, Claudia would probably answer the phone—and no way could she tell Claudia what was happening.

She was standing staring into space when, at that precise moment, the telephone rang, and Mornay jumped like a scalded cat. In the next second, however, with thoughts of Gerry, Claudia and the telephone still in her mind, she was diving into the sitting-room to answer it.

To her horror, however, she made it to the sitting-room just in time to see Brad Kendrick in the act of picking it up. Worse, as she went to grab it from him—knowing that she was going to be hard put to it to explain why some strange man should be answering her phone, be the caller either Claudia, Gerry or indeed, Mr Probert—so the man who was using her home like

Liberty Hall, and who saw nothing wrong in answering her phone, was saying, 'Hello?'

Ready to snatch the phone from him, Mornay went forward to do just that when he suddenly put an arm out to bar her way. Then said, 'Ah, Helen, what have you got for me?'

Abruptly Mornay let her hands fall back to her sides, and as she saw him reach for the pencil and telephone pad and then start to make notes she began to fume, Trust him to have the most efficient secretary ever created!

She thereafter tried to ignore him as she realised that for the caller to have been either Claudia or Gerry, they would first have had to have telephoned her office and have discovered that she wasn't in work yet. When that thought began to trigger off even more horrendous thoughts—such as Mr Probert ringing Claudia to find out what was wrong with his secretary that she wasn't in work, and the consequences of that—Mornay decided that she would rather listen in to what Brad Kendrick was saying.

She tuned in as, giving his secretary a few business instructions, he then terminated the call by telling her, 'And, Helen—leave it twenty-four hours before you announce to anyone interested that I'm recuperating abroad.'

Mornay had time only for it to register that he really did value his privacy, then he was putting the phone down and had his eyes on her. He was starting to look tired again, she saw, though there was nothing tired about his voice when he addressed her. For his tone was firm and authoritative when, 'Are you packed?' he clipped.

'Packed?' Mornay queried, her thoughts more on how he looked as though a lie-down might do him more good than anything.

She was rapidly brought to earth, however, when he grunted tersely, 'If we're to make Scotland before nightfall, we'd better get started.'

CHAPTER FIVE

A CHILL struck at Mornay's heart. This was it, then—
he hadn't been joking! She looked at him and saw that,
for all he looked bone-weary, he still managed to wear
a 'not to be argued with' look. Biting back a torrent of
heated argument which threatened to burst forth anyway,
she turned swiftly about and returned to her bedroom.

As she threw some of her belongings into a case her
mood swung from being hotly furious, to one of defiance
which said, damn him, she wouldn't go, then to one of
defeat. She had to go and, when it came down to the
nitty gritty, she knew that she had no choice but to go
with him.

In between time, though, while she was fretting and
fuming and finally accepting, Mornay was desperately
wondering what she was going to do about letting
Claudia know where she was—or, as the case might be—
not letting her know where she was. As she loved her
sister, so her sister loved her. Claudia would worry herself
silly if, without explanation, more than a few days went
by with her not making contact. Visualising her sister's
hurt as day after day went by and she did not appear at
Penny Dale to view the new baby, Mornay grew yet more
desperate to know what to do.

It was out of that sheer desperation, however, that the
answer came to her. She was just visualising a whole
hornet's nest being stirred up if, say by tomorrow,
Claudia had thought it peculiar that she had not been
over, and rang her work, only to find out from Mr
Probert that he had not seen anything of her since
Wednesday evening. For sure, Claudia would be getting

Gerry to drive her to her flat on the instant. Mornay had just gone into visions of her sister's calling out the police when suddenly she thought—unless . . . and then she had it.

She was uncertain how long she would be away, but if Brad Kendrick insisted that the payment for her 'crime' be *a whole month* of looking after him, then she had packed a fairly large suitcase.

He was still on the couch when, toting her case, she entered the sitting-room. His eyes were closed, she noted, as though he was intent on getting what rest he could before the start of their journey. She flicked a glance to the phone and, guessing that beneath those closed lids he was not asleep, she was tempted to take the phone into the kitchen.

Her glance flicked to his bruised left wrist, the source of her present inspiration—her mother was left-handed—and she picked up the phone and dialled the Town Hall from where she was. What did she care? Let Bradford Kendrick know of the lies he had driven her to.

'Mr Probert, please,' she requested when her call was answered and, when put through to him, 'I'm so sorry to be ringing you this late,' she apologised, and then launched, not very comfortably, she had to admit, into how she was phoning from Solihull because her mother had sprained her wrist very badly and very much needed her to assist at her home for a while. 'I was wondering,' she ended, having presented him with a *fait accompli*, 'if I could have some time off out of my holiday allowance.'

She came off the phone renewing her previously held opinion of what a nice man Mr Probert was, for he had sounded more concerned that her mother's wrist would soon heal, when he could very easily have been most disgruntled at having to find a temporary secretary at such short notice. She had hated lying to him, though, but she felt that in that one call she had covered two possibilities. The possibility of Mr Probert's taking it into his head to ring Claudia when his secretary hadn't contacted him had been eliminated, as had the possibility of Claudia's contacting the police if she rang the office and spoke to him. From what Mornay knew of her sister, she felt that she could safely bet that, while Claudia might think her crazy to go dashing over to Solihull at a moment's notice, the one thing she could be fairly certain of was that she would not ring her mother. All that Mornay hoped was that, if her mother had not penned the letter which she had said she would write to Claudia, she did not take it into her head to do it today.

Mornay was just realising that, whatever happened, she must somehow or other get in touch with Gerry as soon as she could, when she suddenly became aware of a pair of dark eyes surveying her.

She was unused to telling lies, and guilt, she supposed, was the reason for her snappiness when, ignoring that his glance seemed to be taking in each of her delicate features in turn, she abruptly erupted, 'Thanks to you, Mr Kendrick, I'm now a liar!'

'Why thank me, Miss Haynes?' he drawled, his glance coming away from her mouth to look her in the eyes. 'If my memory is anywhere as near as good as it used to be, I'd say you were—without any prompting from me—lying your head off before now; within the first five minutes of our speaking to each other, in fact.'

More than ever wishing that she had never invented witnessing an ambulance coming for him after the accident, Mornay had to acknowledge the truth of what he said. That did not stop her from glaring at him just the same when, assuming that he had driven to Reefingham initially, and that he would want them to use his car, she questioned reluctantly, 'Do I have to go to the hotel you were staying in to pick up your car, or what?'

'Or what,' he replied shortly. 'When I contacted the Belvedere I told them to garage it for me until I either collect it or send for it.'

'What you're really saying is that you don't trust me to drive your car, isn't it?' she flared, and when he gave her a cool look as though to say that, if that was what he meant, he would have said it, she added tartly, 'It's a wonder to me that you're trusting me to drive you at all!'

'You can be sure if you hit anything that I'll be hauling you off to the nearest police station to report it,' he silenced her grittily, and Mornay, giving him a look of disdain for his trouble, picked up her case and went to the door.

At the door, however, she halted. Confound it, the man wasn't well, and as she turned and saw the stiff way he got up from the couch she realised that she could be more of a help to him than she was being.

'If you'd like to start on your way down the stairs,' she conquered her crossness to suggest, 'I'll bring your case.'

'I'm quite capable of carrying my own case,' he told her, his disdain beating hers into a cocked hat.

'Suit yourself!' she told him pithily, but was more fed up than angry when, fiddling about with the door lock when inner sensitivity hinted that it wouldn't be so obvious that she was waiting if she looked busy, she hung about while he collected his case and then joined her by the door.

Once her flat had been secured she went on a little way in front of him, her feet slowing at the bottom of the stairs so that it was together that they walked to where she had garaged her Metro.

Placing her case down on the tarmac, she left him standing by it while she unlocked the garage and drove her car out. Though on leaving the driving seat prior to stowing her luggage on board she caught him glancing cold-eyed at the dent in the wing.

'That's one you won't be claiming on your insurance!' he remarked sourly. 'Though, knowing you, I wouldn't put it past you!' he grunted.

'You know nothing about me!' Mornay flared, and received a cynical look from him for her trouble.

She had put her luggage in the boot and he had come round to the hatch and handed her his when she saw that he was looking a degree grey again, and suddenly her heart went out to him.

'Are you sure you're up to this?' she enquired, as yet having no idea of their exact destination but, at a quick calculation, guessing that it was going to take anything up to four hours just to reach the Scottish borders.

But his mockery was back, and despite his looking far from well there was nothing wrong with his tongue when, 'You care?' he drawled.

'Enough to hit every pot-hole!' she erupted, and, slamming the hatch down hard, she locked it and stormed to the driver's seat.

'Swine' was too nice a name for him—that was her considered opinion when, with Brad Kendrick beside her, she drove away from her garage and away from Reefingham and headed north.

Instinctively, however, she did avoid the pot-holes, and, for all she called herself weak for doing it, she drove with care so that no sudden movement would cause the aches in his body to protest more than they must be doing already.

She only realised that she had simmered down from being angry, however, when she noticed that her thinking was going along the path of not really blaming him, when she remembered him looking at the dent in her wing, and thought about the evidence *he* had, for not wanting her to drive his car. A few minutes later, and she found she had gone on to consider that maybe he wasn't so much bothered about his car but—since it appeared that he was a person who very much valued his privacy—that he was taking the precaution of not having his car recognised, his whereabouts pin-pointed—by using hers.

She had told him that he knew nothing of her, but there was, she considered, a tremendous amount that she did not know about him. It was around then that Mornay decided that, since it seemed she could not get out of going to Scotland with him—for, had there been a chance, she would not be with him now, heading that way—she was going to make the best of it. She had heard him laugh once, she recalled, so things couldn't be all bad. And for him to have laughed at all when he must be feeling as off-colour as he looked just had to be a plus—didn't it?

She took a sideways glance at him, and, seeing that his eyes were open, 'Where are we making for?' she asked him quietly, her tone affable.

'A place called Kilcaber in Renfrewshire,' he obliged in an even voice.

'Do you know it?'

'I've never been there,' he admitted, and added, 'We'll buy a map when we stop for petrol.'

Mornay was doing all she knew how to 'make the best of things' when not long afterwards they did have to stop for petrol. She came close to an involuntary eruption, however, when as she went to pay for the purchase she found that Brad, who had gone into the shop-cum-paying-area, had settled what was due at the same time as he had paid for a map he had selected.

Biting back her independent streak, she returned to her car, and when he got into the passenger seat she drove off the garage forecourt. He had decided to take a look at the map when, an hour later, thinking that his aching body must sorely be in need of a rest, Mornay decided to stop.

She stopped outside a huge motorway restaurant, and when he looked at her questioningly she lied, 'I need a rest,' and might have got away with that lie, had she not—in her search for tact—forgotten how quick-thinking he could be when she didn't want him to be. 'Do you feel up to having a meal?' she enquired with the best tact she could muster. 'Or shall I get something for us to eat going along?'

'Far be it from me to deprive *you* of your rest,' he replied coolly. He it was, then, who led the way into the restaurant.

They were seated in the restaurant however when, no matter what his private opinion of her might be, Mornay discovered that there was no way he would deliberately embarrass her in public. For when, if she had thought at all, she would have thought that he would either have ignored her, or, at the very least—especially in the instance of him not feeling so good—replied sharply to anything she had to say, he did nothing of the kind.

'Do you like your work?' he enquired when, he having ordered a curry while she opted for a salad, they were seated waiting for their meals.

'Driving?' she asked, her tone suspicious.

'Secretarial,' he replied, and suddenly smiled a gentle smile that sent her suspicions flying.

Just then the waitress came and Mornay, having chosen salad mainly because it was such a blisteringly hot day, watched as Brad picked up his fork. After telling him, 'Yes, I quite like my work,' she could not deny an inquisitiveness which she discovered she had about him when, in view of the baking heat, she just had to add, 'As you like curry.'

'Curry?' he replied, then, looking down to his plate, he actually grinned as he shrugged and revealed, 'It was about the only thing on the menu that I thought I could manage one-handed.'

'Oh, Brad!' escaped her involuntarily, as she guiltily realised that, after seeing the way he'd had difficulty at breakfast time, she should have been aware of his problems. 'I should have thought——'

'When I want you to cut my meat up for me, I'll let you know,' he interrupted, but there was still a trace of a smile about his most agreeably shaped mouth, she observed.

The day had started to cloud over when, back in the car again, they headed further north. Though it was still quite warm when, after an hour and a half of driving, Mornay considered that it might be an idea if she stopped to allow him to stretch a few of the creaks out of his body.

'I'm gasping for a cup of tea,' she lied. 'Joining me?' she queried as she drew the car to a halt.

'Wouldn't dream of disappointing you,' he murmured, and Mornay realised that quite plainly he had seen straight through her.

They stayed idling over a pot of tea for a good half-hour, and as before Brad Kendrick remained pleasant, and had no harsh comment to make that might have made her feel uncomfortable.

In fact so pleasant was he that, for all she was hoping against hope that a busy businessman such as him would get fed up with his Scottish exile well before the month he'd stipulated was up, she had started to think that maybe the time she had to spend looking after him might not be so completely untenable as she'd first feared.

They were back in the car and were motoring on when her new-found curiosity about him made her want to question what he had been doing in her part of the world that fateful night. She should, she later realised, have kept her curiosity to herself, but since his pleasant manner seemed to be still about him she plunged in— where angels feared to tread.

'Do you come to Reefingham often?' she queried, apropos of nothing.

'If you're thinking that when you've "nursed me back to full health" I shall again call on you—forget it!' he suddenly, and unfairly, she thought, snarled.

'The saints forbid!' she flared, wondering where the even-tempered being she had been before knowing him had gone; since knowing him, she had found she could go from calm to furious in less time than it took to blink. 'It's to be hoped that I never have to see you again! You can be darn sure that I'd quickly run the other way if I saw you coming!' she raced on angrily. 'It's——'

'Which is what I should have done,' he sliced in to chop her off. 'Foolish of me to suppose you would stop at a red traffic signal,' he added sarcastically.

The rest of the journey was completed in stony silence. Nothing in creation would have made Mornay speak to the vile creature again. When they reached Renfrewshire, she stopped the car and, without deigning to put a single question to him, leaned over and helped herself to the map, located the Kilcaber he had spoken of, and drove on.

She was feeling not one whit friendlier towards him when she saw the signpost saying that they had arrived at Kilcaber. Again she stopped the car, and again she said not a word. This time, however, she just sat perfectly still. It did not take but a moment for Brad Kendrick to catch on. In seconds, he had given her the address she was to drive to.

Mornay's spirits were in no way lifted when, arriving at the address he had given her, she saw that, though it was not a discreet hotel, neither was it a quiet boarding house—nor a house at all, for that matter. But, stuck in the back of beyond, the hideaway they had come to was a small, if modern-looking, bungalow.

More made speechless than not intending to speak, Mornay got out of the car and, not at all certain what

she had been expecting anyway, she realised that his
secretary had probably obeyed his instructions to the
letter. You couldn't, she thought dully, get more hidden
away than here!

'Are you going to stand there staring forever, or are
you going to unlock the boot so I can get my case?'

Mornay turned about and saw that Brad was out of
the car and that he was waiting by the back of her vehicle. She tossed him a look of intense dislike, but went
and opened up the boot, and was human enough to hope
it hurt him when—too impatient to wait for her to hand
his case out—he stretched inside to get it.

'I'll carry my own case!' she snapped when, as though
to prove that it had not pained him at all, he went to
lift out her much larger case, automatically, it seemed.

'Why shouldn't you?' he snarled, and left her to it.
Mornay was struggling up the path to a month's pur-
gatory with her case when suddenly the door to the
bungalow opened and a pleasant-faced sandy-haired lady
emerged, wearing a floral overall.

'I heard the car,' she greeted Brad, not yet seeing
Mornay who was passing behind an overgrown rhodo-
dendron bush. 'Come away in,' she beamed, in a beautiful Scottish accent, 'everything's ready for you!'
Mornay's depressed spirits had lifted a few degrees that,
by the look of it, she was not stuck with just that swine
of a man for company, but that there was a resident
housekeeper, when, 'Oh, gracious!' the woman declared, as she suddenly spotted Mornay. 'They didn't
say that you'd be bringing your wife!'

Wife! Mornay neared the door and was about to set
the woman straight without delay, but she did not get
the chance—for there was too much else going on.
Somehow or other they were all standing in the small
hall with the outer door closed and the sandy-haired lady
was introducing herself as Mrs Macdonald, and was
addressing them as Mr and Mrs Adams. About to again

try and interrupt to say that she was not married to the brute she had the misfortune to accompany, Mornay was distracted as she realised that his secretary had excelled herself when, in finding him his hideaway, she had also found him a name with which no one would associate him.

With the moment gone when she could have put Mrs Macdonald right, Mornay tuned back in to wonder why she should bother putting her right, and to hear that the woman was not the live-in housekeeper but was a lady who occasionally worked for the renting agent. She had apparently been called in to come and air the bungalow, purchase some provisions, and to prepare a simple meal for when a Mr Adams arrived that day.

'I didn't know what time you'd arrive, but because it's turned chilly I thought a casserole would be about the best. It's in the oven now,' Mrs Macdonald informed them, but fretted, 'But I don't know that it'll be enough for two.'

'I'm sure it will be, Mrs Macdonald,' Brad assured her, his charm, in view of his attitude five minutes earlier, startling Mornay. She was startled again when, not a second later, he went on, 'My wife and I ate a substantial lunch on the way here, so a small portion of casserole each will be ideal.'

'If you're sure...' Mrs Macdonald began, but had her smile flushed out by him, and when he asked how much was he in her debt, replied, 'I've put the receipts for what I bought on the kitchen table.' It seemed only polite to Mornay that she should leave her case in the hall and follow Brad and the woman into the kitchen.

Looking round the kitchen while 'Mr Adams' thanked Mrs Macdonald for seeing to things so well, and settled all accounts with her, Mornay observed that the kitchen was absolutely spotless.

'There's bacon, eggs, butter and milk in the fridge, and bread in the bin,' the woman who was such a tidy

worker drew Mornay's gaze. 'And I've left my telephone number on the pad next to your phone, should
you need me for anything,' she went on. And while
Mornay registered gratefully that the out of the way
bungalow had a phone—though when and how she was
going to get to use it to ring Gerry in private was another
matter—the wiry-looking woman was adding that she
lived but a mile down the road.

Mornay's gaze was then drawn to Brad when he courteously passed the time of day with the woman as she
collected her basket and cardigan from a chair and edged
towards the outer kitchen door. He was looking quite
exhausted again, she saw, and, as he went with Mrs
Macdonald and opened the door for her, so all Mornay's
animosity against him suddenly died.

'Goodbye, Mr Adams—goodbye, Mrs Adams,' Mrs
Macdonald smiled.

'Goodbye—and thank you,' Mornay smiled back, and
had more on her mind than to explain her single status.
From the kitchen window she saw Mrs Macdonald cycle
off down the road, then Mornay addressed the man
whom not long ago she'd have bitten her tongue rather
than speak to. 'If I may say so, Mr Adams,' she voiced
quietly, 'I'd say that you'd be better off in bed.'

He looked across at her, his expression unsmiling, and
she rather guessed that she was in for a repeated snarled
earful along the lines that he'd had enough of bed. But,
to her surprise, his reply was not snarled, nor was it in
any way what she expected. But, 'If I may say so, Mrs
Adams,' he replied, his tone as quiet as hers had been,
'you're something else again.' Quite what that was supposed to mean, Mornay wasn't sure, though she had an
idea that it might have something to do with the fact
that she seemed to be accepting a situation when she
must have realised that there was not a thing she could
otherwise do. He did not, however, take up her suggestion that he'd be better off in bed but decreed, 'Let's

take a look round,' and was on his way to the door that
led to the hall.

Mornay's respect for Helen Boulter went up in bounds
when she realised that his secretary must have worked
out that it might be better, in view of the trauma his
body had received, for him to live on one level rather
than have to climb stairs. Mornay had no complaints
about the furnishings either. The sitting-room, which she
quickly espied housed the telephone, was thickly carpeted, had fresh linen curtains, a quite luxurious-looking
three-piece suite, a television and a couple of highly pol-
ished occasional tables, as well as some quite liveable-
with pictures adorning one wall.

'So far, so good,' Brad commented.

The bungalow had a separate dining-room, and two
bedrooms, both of which, in addition to the normal
bedroom furniture, had a double bed, though only one
of the beds had been made up.

'Which room do you want?' he gave her the choice
as they stood in the room which Mrs Macdonald had
made ready.

'You have this one,' Mornay replied, and dared, considering that he seemed to be rocking on his feet, to
suggest, 'Why don't you get into bed now—it's been a
long day for you? I could bring your supper in on a
tray.'

'You're too good to me,' he mocked. His eyes went
to the bed. 'Give me a shout around eight,' he told her.

Mornay left him hoping that he would at least lie down
on top of his bed and have a rest, and went looking for
the airing cupboard. In no time at all she had rooted
out sheets, pillow-slips and a light blanket for the bed
in the room she would have, and, moving quietly so as
not to disturb the man in the room next door, she set
about making up her bed and doing some unpacking.

At a quarter to eight she was in the middle of laying
the dining-room table when Brad came and joined her.

She saw at once that he had more colour in his face, but
not all that much.

'I was going to give you a call,' she told him.

'I've saved you the bother.'

She wanted to ask him if he'd managed to snatch a
nap, but thought he might resent it. 'Have you taken
your tablets?' she asked instead, adding hurriedly, 'Shall
I get you some water?'

'I've taken them without,' he said easily. 'Can I do
anything?'

'You can sit there,' she told him, a shade bossily, she
had to admit. But to her surprise she saw him go and
meekly take the chair she had indicated at the table.
Before she left the room though, she glanced at his face
and could have sworn that he was holding back a grin.

Now what had amused him? she wondered as she went
to the kitchen and cut some bread to add bulk to their
meal. Had it amused him that she should take it upon
herself to boss him around—or was he amusing himself
by humouring her and allowing her to give him orders?

'This is good,' he remarked when, insisting that the
casserole be divided into two equal portions when she
attempted to give him the lion's share, they sat opposite
each other tucking in to Mrs Macdonald's excellent
cooking.

'It is,' Mornay agreed, but very little else was remarked
upon during the meal.

Though she was pleased to see that he had a good
appetite. If his appetite stayed with him then day by day
he would gain more and more strength. Mornay hoped
that it was not wishful thinking on her part, but she felt
that all looked fair for an early return to their respective
homes.

'Have you had enough?' she enquired when he laid
down his fork.

'Ample,' he replied.

'Mrs Macdonald has left an apple pie——'

'No, thanks,' he butted in, and Mornay's hopes for an early getaway took a dip.

She wanted quite badly then to tell him that he must eat, but, looking into his tired eyes, she refrained. 'Why don't you go and have an early night?' she suggested instead, and then found that, just as she was scrutinising his face, so he was scrutinising hers.

'You look as though an early night wouldn't come amiss with you, for that matter,' he observed.

It did not surprise Mornay that she looked a wreck, though she did not thank him for referring to it. She started to clear the table, of the opinion that, since she had barely slept on Monday night, and on Tuesday night for that matter, and that since one night on her couch last night was one night too many, the only wonder was that she didn't have bags under her eyes stretching down to her knees.

When, reaching for the cruet, she suddenly saw Brad reach for it at the same time, she realised that he was helping her to clear away—but she didn't thank him for that either.

In all honesty, she could not say that he was in a talkative frame of mind when he came into the kitchen and did the best his bruised wrists would allow to help with the washing-up. Thankfully, however, Mrs Macdonald had washed up after her cooking, and there was little of it to do.

Mornay had formed the opinion, as she cast a last tidying, inspecting eye around the kitchen, that she would be going to bed without another word passing between her and Bradford Kendrick.

But she was proved wrong about that. For, as she went to walk past him on her way out of the kitchen, she distinctly heard him comment, 'Cheer up—it might never happen!'

'Goodnight,' she said as civilly as she could muster, and carried on walking, not stopping until she was inside her bedroom with the door closed.

There it was that she sank down on her bed and sighed heavily. 'Cheer up,' he'd said. How could she? Here she was in Kilcaber, Renfrewshire with a man she had no liking for—and who certainly had no liking for her. What was there to be cheerful about, when she didn't want to be here but back in Reefingham? Or, more precisely, since she had a baby nephew she hadn't even seen yet, back in Penny Dale. At least in Penny Dale she would be with people who loved her.

CHAPTER SIX

ODDLY, Mornay slept exceptionally well that night, and awakened on Friday morning feeling much better about her situation than she had on going to bed.

Being careful not to disturb her 'patient', she went very quietly along to the bathroom, bathed and dressed in cotton trousers and, in view of the change in the weather, a lightweight long-sleeved sweater.

Then she returned to her room and brushed her long blonde hair prior to pinning it back in a simple plait which ended halfway between her shoulder-blades. By that time she was seeing nothing at all odd in the fact that she had slept so soundly last night. What would have been odd, she reflected, bearing in mind her scant sleep of the three previous nights, would be any chance she had of staying awake!

Mornay had left her room and had gone silently to the kitchen when she wondered what in thunder had come over her last night, that she had wanted to be loved—or at least be with people who loved her. Now that was odd, if you liked. Most odd.

She began opening cupboards and taking a mental inventory when, feeling so very much better-humoured for a good night's sleep, she determined that if her time with *him* had to be endured, then she would endure it in a more cheerful—yes, cheerful, mood.

Which was the reason why, when the kitchen door opened half an hour later and a clean-shaven Brad Kendrick walked in, she greeted him with a bright, 'Good morning!'

'Somebody obviously slept well,' he observed.

'How did you sleep?' she enquired, her eyes scanning his face as he came further into the kitchen. She was sure he was looking much more rested and a degree or two improved, but looks could be deceiving.

'Went out like a light,' he replied.

'Have you taken your pills?' she queried, and was made to suffer his baleful stare for her trouble.

'Hell take it!' he breathed. 'Are you going to go on bleating in this demented nanny fashion for the whole of our stay?'

'So don't take them—see if I care!' she sniffed huffily, and nearly died when, as the funny side of it hit her and her lips twitched, his sense of humour came out and met hers halfway and, against all odds, they were suddenly both laughing.

'So what's for breakfast?' he enquired when, the first to sober, he took his glance from the sweet curve of her mouth.

'I thought boiled eggs,' she replied, and then queried, 'How long are we staying?'

'Homesick already?' he rapped, his tone hostile and sounding every bit as though he resented that she had—briefly—had the power to make him laugh. 'Or,' he went on when she stared crossly at this change in him, 'is it that you're homesick for your boyfriend?'

Mornay tossed him a 'give me strength' look, and forced herself to remember that she had determined to endure her time with him more cheerfully. He must still ache here and there, she reminded herself, although by then she was under no illusion that one Bradford Kendrick was the best patient in the world.

'How could I possibly be homesick?' she bit back a hot retort to tell him sweetly. She waved an airy hand around as if pointing out the splendid isolation. 'Haven't you "brought me away from it all"'?'

For a moment she thought she saw a smile trying to get through, but if it was he suppressed it. 'If you prefer, we can always drive to the police station,' he murmured silkily.

Mornay glared at him, not missing the underlying threat that one step out of line from her and he'd be hauling her off to the police station to make a full confession.

'How long do you like you eggs boiled?' she snapped.

'How the devil do I know?' he tossed back.

Clearly, he was a man who had never had to look after himself. 'We'll breakfast in here,' she told him, feeling sour enough to consider that it wouldn't hurt him to grow more familiar with what a kitchen looked like, and saw him shrug, it being apparently all the same to him where they breakfasted.

Strangely, however, as they sat across the table from each other, breakfasting on boiled eggs and bread and butter, she discovered that her thinking was dominated by the question of—who normally cooked for him? He wasn't married, she knew that. Did he have a live-in girl-friend? Mornay pondered that for some time, and came to the conclusion that surely, if he felt that deeply about any female, that female would be the one to be with him now.

'Something bothering you?'

Brad's voice suddenly penetrated, and Mornay blushed startled. 'I—er . . .' she murmured before she had got her thoughts together. 'If we're staying longer than today, I need to go shopping,' she told him.

'I'll come with you,' he at once stated.

Mornay stared at him, and was wide-eyed and innocent as she aloofly asked, 'You usually accompany your housekeeper when she goes into town shopping for provisions?'

He shook he head. 'But then, neither do I take Mrs Greaves with me when I go into town shopping for a change of linen.'

Mornay smiled, and even though she acknowledged that it was most peculiar, she realised that she was quite glad to know that he had a housekeeper. 'You're not worried that you might be recognised?' she queried.

'You're saying you want to go out on your own?' he questioned shortly.

'You must be getting better!' Mornay snapped. 'Or are you always such an irritable brute? It was you who wanted a "hideaway", not me!' she reminded him heatedly.

'No one around here will know Mr Adams from Jock,' he took the heat out of her by saying lightly. 'Unless you tell them differently,' he added, then spoiled it all by adding pleasantly, 'Which, of course, you won't.' Mornay glared at him, sensing the threat behind his words, and as she saw him transfer some stray eggshell from the table to his plate she hoped he grew warts. But she was mollified completely when he went on, 'But I've got double cover,' and, when she looked coldly at him without comment, 'Our friend Adams has a beautiful wife—Kendrick has no wife at all.'

Mornay bent her head as she got up from her chair and began to clear the table, and was certain that she wasn't at all flattered that, for a second time, Brad Kendrick had intimated that he thought her beautiful.

Again he helped her with the washing-up and, thinking that to dry a few dishes might be some kind of physiotherapy for his wrists, Mornay let him. Then, 'I'll just go and make your bed and tidy your room, then——'

'I've made my bed,' he interrupted.

'Then we'll go shopping,' she told him.

For all the skies had clouded over, there was no sign of rain, and it was still quite warm when Mornay drove into Kilcaber. There were two shops in the village—neither of which could even loosely be called a 'Gentleman's Outfitters'.

'I'd better drive on,' she told Brad.

'What have we got to lose?' he replied, and seemed so content somehow to while the day away that Mornay suddenly had the oddest notion that he was starting to enjoy himself. That, there being nothing else for it, he had accepted the situation which being badly shaken up in an accident had caused, and was now—like her—making the best of it.

She was not terribly sure about what her intelligence had brought her, though, for she would have supposed that a man of his obvious sophistication would find little that was pleasurable in trundling along in an Austin Metro on his way to get the groceries and a couple of clean shirts. But suddenly she was feeling choked by an emotion which she could not define. 'Brad,' she involuntarily said his name, and when he looked at her she took her eyes off the road for a moment and turned her head, 'I'm sorry,' she said, and when he said not a word and she looked to the front again, she realised that her apology for being in her car that fateful night had been long overdue.

Mornay parked the Metro in the first town she came to that housed a supermarket and a men's clothiers, but as she got out of the car she was very much conscious of the fact that Brad still had some way to go yet to full recovery. His comment at breakfast about her 'bleating like a demented nanny', however, was in her mind too, so that when the impulse came to tell him to wait there while she went to the supermarket she held it down.

That did not stop her from keeping a watchful eye on him, even if she did pretend to be very much absorbed in the variety of ties on a tie display in the clothiers while Brad purchased everything he would need from the skin out.

'We'll take a trolley,' she told him at the supermarket, and, thinking that if he was tired that he could lean his weight on it as they went round, she told him, 'and you can push it.'

'You'll make someone a lovely sergeant-major,' he murmured.

'Shut up,' she told him.

He was, she discovered, an extravagant shopper. Either that or, shopping in a supermarket new to him, he found pleasure in lifting things down off the shelves, examining them, and dropping them in the trolley. Or, she realised, he was laying up stocks for a whole month's siege.

The thought of a month away from her job, from Reefingham and without a word to Claudia, who would surely turn her back on her principles and phone their mother if she hadn't heard from her in a whole month, caused Mornay to come close to panic again. Her panic did not stay around for long, though, for something else was dropped into the trolley and she just had to ask, 'What, for crying out loud, do we want dried apricots for?'

'Humour me,' he told her, and, looking up into his dark eyes, Mornay could see laughter dancing there as he added, 'I've not been well.'

What could she do? She burst out laughing and helped him to push the trolley to the checkout. Fortunately, since neither of them was equipped to carry a ton of shopping, the supermarket had a system whereby they could collect their purchases from the rear of the store and have them loaded directly into the car.

Fortunately, too, there was a wealth of empty cupboard space when they unloaded the car at the other end. 'Have you a preference for lunch?' Mornay asked when, because he wouldn't have it otherwise, she'd had to give way and allow him to carry the heaviest of the boxes in.

'Anything will suit,' he replied, and sounded so indifferent to what he ate that Mornay could not help but feel a degree of anxiety that his appetite seemed to have disappeared. She was therefore much cheered, however, when a moment later he commented, 'Though whatever we're having, can you make mine king-size?'

Realising that a boiled egg for breakfast was hardly likely to sustain more than a corner of his tall broad-shouldered manliness, she decided that, because of the difficulty he was still experiencing using a knife and fork, that they would have poached haddock for lunch. Brad could fill up on the delicious-looking apple pie Mrs Macdonald had made, and, Mornay thought, they'd have a more substantial meal for dinnertime when she'd have more time.

She was pouring milk into a saucepan when she began to wonder why she should worry whether his appetite had returned or whether it hadn't. Only a second later, she knew that anyone would have to be particularly heartless not to worry. It was only natural that she should be concerned, for goodness' sake—she was partly to blame for the state he was in. Anyhow, she concluded, the sooner he was fit, the sooner she could go home.

'Have you had sufficient?' she queried when, after a second helping of apple pie, Brad laid down his spoon.

'Plenty—it was delicious,' he said. 'All of it,' he qualified, just as though he knew that she was about to disclaim any credit for the apple pie. 'Who taught you the intricacies of slaving over a hot stove?' he brought a smile to her face by asking.

'My mother,' Mornay owned, and was so taken that he seemed to be semi-teasing her that she went on, quite unthinkingly, 'My sister and I...er——' she faltered and, there being nothing for it if she was not to draw his attention to what she considered a most gigantic gaffe '—both learned to cook from an early age.'

'How old are you now?' he enquired, and Mornay inwardly drew a sigh of relief that she was over that hurdle without his asking more about her sister.

'Twenty-two,' she answered.

'With that pigtail,' he smiled, and twisted to the side so he could see it, 'you look about sixteen.'

'I like it,' she defended her plait.

'Did I say I didn't?' he queried, and Mornay experienced the most peculiar tingling sensation that he must be saying that he liked something about her.

'The newspaper said you were thirty-six,' she said hastily. 'Did they get it right?'

'For once,' he replied, but suddenly any sign of friendliness in him had gone—and Mornay knew she was to blame.

She began to clear the dining-room table, and went to the kitchen reflecting that she should be used by now to the way Brad's attitude cooled whenever anything remotely connected with that car accident came up. That report about him would never have been in the paper had her car not knocked him down—and plainly, being reminded of the accident brought back to him her guilt in it all.

Mornay washed dishes at the sink and with her thoughts on the newspaper article she again remembered—and wished that she hadn't—that it had stated how no man ever put one over on him without living to regret it. She swallowed hard as she thought of the one she was putting over on him in that it was her brother-in-law, and not she, who had knocked him down.

At that moment Brad entered the kitchen and she flicked a glance to his grim-looking expression. She somehow knew that his thoughts were on the accident too, and felt then that the best she could hope for was that he never discovered the truth.

Which thought made her jumpy when he came near, and before she could stop herself she had snapped, 'I'll do that!' when she saw him reach for the tea-towel.

'Please yourself!' he gritted, his arm falling back to his side, but to her displeasure he did not go from the room but took a seat on one of the kitchen chairs.

Mornay carried on with her chores, not glancing his way once, but wondering all the while if he was watching her or, with his long legs stretched out in front of him, was studying his toes.

When the tea-towel was hung up to dry and, having wiped down all the surfaces, she had draped the dish-cloth over the washing-up bowl, Mornay, on her way out of the kitchen, did take a glance at him. Was it the light, she pondered, or was he not looking as improved as he had at breakfast?

Whether he was or not, however, she suddenly discovered that it was just impossible for her to walk by without a word. 'Why don't...?' she began, but the words to suggest that he go and rest for an hour or two on his bed were suddenly beaten back by the memory of his 'demented nanny' comment that morning. Which, since she had stopped bang in front of him and was standing looking into a pair of disagreeable dark eyes, left her with little alternative but to snap aggressively, 'Are you going to sit there all day?'

She saw his eyes narrow, and, catching a glimpse of the ice that was starting to form as his aggression came out to meet hers, she was hard put to it not to swallow on a suddenly dry mouth. Then he was standing up, and from his superior height he was looking down his superior nose and barking aggressively, 'No! I'm going for a walk, and you're coming with me!'

Mornay had no intention of going for a walk, or so she thought. But that was before she remembered that he had the upper hand—and she knew then that she was in no position to do other than to jump to his black-mailing bidding. Stubbornly hostile, though, she stared mutinously up at him. Then, to her annoyance, when she saw that he did indeed seem to have lost some of his earlier improved colour, her mutiny began to fold. She had no idea how far he intended to walk but from the look of him somebody had to go with him, if only to make sure that he got safely back.

But, 'Who,' she snapped, not wanting him to think she was going under anything but protest, 'could resist such an invitation, *and* one so charmingly put?'

Their walk was not overlong, nor was it filled with scintillating conversation, for just as she had nothing she wanted to say to him, so he, it soon became apparent, had nothing he wanted to say to her.

And so it continued for most of the weekend. Mornay coped as best she could with her inner anxieties about getting back to Reefingham before her sister rang her parents' home in Solihull to enquire why her mother's sprained wrist was taking so long to heal, and in between times set about making the most delicious meals to tempt Brad Kendrick's appetite.

But by Monday, although his health seemed to be tremendously improved in that he was now moving with very little sign of stiffness, and was most definitely looking much better, Mornay had fresh worries on her mind.

How she had come to overlook the fact that, since Robert Naylor knew where her parents lived, he might well telephone them, she couldn't have said. Though in all likelihood it was probably because she had so much else on her mind that, with Robert—up until last Friday—safely away in Wales, it just hadn't occurred to her that her lie to Mr Probert could well reach his ears. If Mr Probert had passed her lie on to Claudia then there was nothing to prevent Mr Probert's or Claudia's passing that lie on to Robert if he rang trying to contact her. Mornay blanched when she realised that, by now, Robert could have phoned her mother to hope that her wrist was mending while at the same time asking to speak to her younger daughter.

'Oh, grief!' Mornay groaned when she got out of bed on Tuesday morning—somehow, she was just going to have to phone Gerry to find out what was happening. Though how she was going to be able to do that with that surly brute Brad Kendrick forever being within earshot, she had no idea.

Or rather, she thought she had no idea. But that was before she'd done an after-breakfast reconnoitre of the kitchen cupboards. In particular she was anxious to note what—of the many purchases made—they did not have.

Brad, his wrists virtually no longer a problem now, was giving a solemn hand with the washing-up and was putting plates away in a dresser while Mornay investigated the plentiful supplies available. They did not have any asparagus, she saw. Nor, in truth, did they actually need any—but the lack of it represented a chance for her to get to a telephone booth.

'We're having smoked salmon and asparagus flan for lunch,' she addressed Brad aloofly over her shoulder, putting all her faith in the hope that his one taste of supermarket shopping had been enough to last him a lifetime. 'I'll have to take the car and get some asparagus,' she added.

She could have happily crowned him when, dealing her high hopes a mortal blow, he loftily replied, 'I'm ready when you are.'

Swine! Mornay dubbed him when, having gone completely off the idea of making a smoked salmon and asparagus flan, she drove, with Brad in the passenger seat, to get the rest of the ingredients to do just that.

She was aware of his brooding silence all the way to the supermarket, just as she was aware that, with him as her shadow, she was not left alone for a minute in which to try and get to a phone.

Which was why she was probably as brooding as him on the homeward journey when, quite suddenly, he abruptly asked, 'How long have you lived in Reefingham?'

Having almost blurted out straight away that she had lived in Reefingham all her life and that he should mind his own business, she suddenly grew wary. She had no idea what—if anything at all—lay behind his question, but with his being so quick on the uptake she thought she might do well to watch anything she told him, no matter how innocent that question might be. So, having made a point of looking in her rear-view mirror as though concentrating on something that was happening behind, 'Er—why do you ask?' she questioned evenly.

From the corner of her eye she saw him shrug as though to say that if she was going to make an issue of it, he wished that he had never asked. 'No particular reason other than idle curiosity as to why you should want to leave your home in Solihull.'

'I've never lived in Sol...' Damn. Feeling intensely irritated with herself that for all her being so wary she had walked straight into that when it was clear that he thought she had moved from Solihull to Reefingham, Mornay had to confess anyway, 'I've lived in Reefingham all my life.'

'Ah,' he said after a moment, 'your family moved to Solihull fairly recently, but you didn't want to move with your parents and sister when they went.'

She felt she could have kissed him for that 'sister' bit, and her heart suddenly lifted, but there was no way she was going to tell him he had made the wrong assumption about her sister. It was far better for him to believe that Claudia lived many miles from Reefingham.

'No,' she replied, and could have added more, but decided that the less she volunteered, the less she had to worry about.

She went on to realise that perhaps his mistake in thinking her sister had moved from the Reefingham area was maybe a natural one in the circumstances of her not having given her a ring to say that she was leaving town. For surely he must be of the opinion that, if she told *anyone* she would not be around for a while, then a sister living locally—if she had one near—would be a far more appropriate person to telephone than even an employer.

Mornay was just taking another relieved breath that it seemed he would never now put two and two together about her sister living so close, or about her sister's having a husband, or any of the rest of it, when, ever a man to question that which needed tidying up, Brad Kendrick put another enquiry.

'Why,' he asked, '*did* you stay behind?'

'I—didn't want to go.'

'Why?'

'You must have driven your mother mad when you were a child!' Mornay snapped, thinking he must have gone around all and every day asking 'Why?'.

'She has the patience of a saint.

'She'd need it!' she said tartly, but, oddly, she felt curiosity begin to stir about his mother. So much so that she almost turned the questioning round to ask him about his family. He, however, got in first.

'Is it such a secret?' he asked.

'What?'

'Your reason for wanting to stay in Reefingham. Don't you get on with your parents?'

'Of course I do!' she snapped stoutly, but suddenly she wanted him off the dangerous subject of her family when who knew, he might start asking questions about her sister. 'It was just that I've got a good job, a good boss——'

'One who's so good that you don't mind lying to him,' Brad cut in coldly, knocking on the head any idea Mornay had that he had started to thaw a little.

'Whose fault is that?' she flared, not thanking him for the reminder that, while he had been in earshot, she had told Mr Probert that awful lie about her mother's sprained wrist.

Brad ignored her question, just as he ignored the reason she chose to give him for staying behind. 'There's some man involved, of course,' he growled.

Mornay was about to deny any such suggestion—then wondered why the dickens she should. 'What if there is?' she questioned, but found that question ignored.

'When did your family move to Solihull?' he wanted to know.

'Wh...it...' Mornay gave a fed-up sigh. 'A couple of years ago!' she answered, becoming resigned, while still wary of some of his questions, to the fact that his 'water wearing away stone' tactics were getting the answers from her that weren't of such great importance.

If she thought, however, that his comments might be done with and that she might be allowed to give her full concentration to her driving—not that there was any traffic around to speak of—then she very quickly was made to realise that she was not going to be allowed to have the last word.

For no sooner had she given him the impression that her major reason for remaining in Reefingham when her family had moved away a couple of years ago was some male of the species than Brad was curtly snarling, 'And you're still a virgin!'

'What the heck has that got to do with anything?' she erupted.

'A hell of a lot, I'd say!' Mornay decided thereafter that she would ignore him, but she had driven only a half a mile further when, 'Do you still see him?' he questioned.

It was on the tip of her tongue to ask what that had to do with him, but she was fast suspecting that when he started out on a course of questioning that sort of a reply would be batted out of the way if he was intent on being answered. She took a deep and restraining breath. 'Regularly,' she told him tightly, and, having hoped that that would shut him up, she was left holding fast on to the steering-wheel—at the next question he found to fire.

'Had you been with him a week ago yesterday when, after your "celebration", we—"met"?' he asked acidly.

'No, I hadn't!' Mornay answered promptly, as she fought not to panic that it seemed he might latch on to the idea any minute now that she had not been alone in her car. 'For your information,' she went on trying to head him swiftly off the scent, 'Robert spent the whole of last week in Wales.'

'Let's hope he didn't spend too much time at the weekend looking for you,' Brad replied silkily, and Mornay could have hit him—she drove the rest of the way to the bungalow in a state of agitation in case Robert, after a call to Claudia, had taken it into his head to ring her mother.

Lunch was eaten in morose silence. Mornay felt she had nothing she wanted to say to Brad—he quite obviously had nothing he wanted to say to her. Which was just lovely, she thought, for if he got fed up enough with her perhaps they could both go home.

The sooner, the better, too, she mused as she washed dishes and he dried them. She then became irritated with herself that she should feel something akin to a small sensation of regret that he plainly took not the minutest bit of pleasure from her company.

For goodness' sake! she inwardly exploded and, impatient with herself, and with the washing-up done, she went without a word to him to the outer door. He had joined her for what was now a habitual after-lunch walk before she had the door open.

After fifteen minutes of walking, she thought they had better turn back. Brad was improving all the time but he still wasn't up to a marathon, she felt. As she expected, he turned about with her, but when they had walked for another five minutes so a weakening appeared in her resolve not to say another word to the wretched man.

Another five minutes further on and she grew conscious that, since he had made that 'demented nanny' crack, she had not once asked him how he was. He looked improved, but, as she had thought before, looks could be very deceiving. Perhaps he was such a miserable devil because despite appearances he was feeling very far from up to the mark.

It was touch and go then that she did not ask him how he was. She did open her mouth as the bungalow hove into view, but fear of a rebuff, and knowing that she was going to feel like hitting him over the head if he made another 'demented nanny'-type crack, caused her to close it again.

She could not resist a quick glance at him, however. But, when she had meant only to check on how well or otherwise he was looking, so as she looked up she saw that he had his glance on her. Hurriedly she looked away, but was certain that he must have seen her open and close her mouth as though she had changed her mind about saying something—that, or she was doing her goldfish impression.

Mornay saw very little of him once they were back in the bungalow. He took himself off to the sitting-room with the newspapers and paperbacks he had purchased while they had been out that morning, while she stayed in the kitchen. She made some cakes, prepared the vegetables for dinner and in between leafed through a couple of magazines she had purchased.

Half an hour before they normally ate, she went into the dining-room intending to lay the table, only to find that Brad had not spent the whole while since she had last seen him with his head stuck in a book.

Somehow, the fact that he had laid the table softened her. She might have got it wrong, but it seemed to her that his attempt to help was a very nice way of saying

'I'm sorry I'm a grouch, but I'm not feeling quite fit yet'.

She consequently felt much more sensitive to him than she might otherwise have done when, the meal ready, she went into the sitting-room and broke her silence of the past six hours. 'Dinner,' she said quietly, and went to the dining-room.

Brad followed her into the room almost immediately, but seemed no more talkative than he had been. But that was all right by her; he had tried to make up for being such a taciturn monster by laying the table, and he couldn't help it if he wasn't well.

When the pudding stage had been reached, however, and barely a word except a request for the pepper had left his lips, Mornay started to wonder if she had got it all wrong after all. Perhaps he'd had no intention of making amends when he'd laid the table—perhaps he'd just been bored with his book.

She flicked a glance to his face, thinking that she might better judge his mood from his expression. But again she found that his glance was on her, and she opened her mouth. This time, however, she felt that to close it without saying anything might give him cause to believe that she was afraid to voice an opinion on anything that came to mind.

'Er—do you know Reefingham well?' she asked the first question to pop into her head, forgetting entirely that the last time she had attempted to question him about what he had been doing in her home town that never-to-be-forgotten Monday she had regretted giving her curiosity its head.

But to her relief, this time, instead of hurling something short and sarcastic at her, he replied civilly enough, 'Not at all,' but pleased her by adding, 'Which is why I motored down the day before a scheduled meeting in connection with some industrial development that might or might not take off.'

'You're thinking of building a factory on the Springfields Industrial Estate?' Mornay cottoned on fast to ask, and felt enormously proud of her brainwork when he nodded.

She was not so pleased a few moments later, however. For, though Brad's glance went from her eager parted lips to her eyes, and she expected that whatever he said next would be said pleasantly, instead he suddenly frowned darkly.

At once Mornay's spirits started to dip, and that was before he toughly stated, 'In view of the millions ultimately involved, I decided to take a look round Reefingham prior to that meeting. I didn't get very far—just as far as from my hotel to a set of traffic lights in the High Street. You,' he accused harshly, 'know the rest.'

Feeling just as though he had physically slapped her, Mornay stared at him in anguish. And then, with her bright blue eyes huge in her face, to her utmost horror she felt the prick of tears at the back of her eyes.

In an instant she was on her feet, but so too was he. Mortified, she felt the shimmer of those tears come to her eyes and abruptly she raced for the door. 'Mornay!' she heard him call, but she was not waiting for anything.

In seconds she had reached the sanctuary of her room. It was many seconds later, though, before she had got herself under control. What for heaven's sake was the matter with her, that he could hurt her so? He was only stating the facts, the facts as he knew them, for goodness' sake. Those same facts that she knew.

Mornay did not venture from her room again that night. She knew full well that the dining-room table was waiting to be cleared. Just as she knew that the washing-up was waiting for her. But the fact that she could easily have burst into tears not so long ago had unnerved her. And since Brad was the cause of that, she was not yet ready to face him again.

She then started to feel that she was his prisoner. True, there were no bars anywhere, and if she cared to leave her room she was free to wander anywhere in the bungalow. Outside of it, though, he was her shadow, she thought glumly.

She went to bed certain that she hated him, and fretted so much about wanting to return to Reefingham, yet knowing that she was forced to stay in Kilcaber until *he* said differently, that it took her an age to get to sleep.

Consequently she overslept the following morning. Indeed, she was sleeping soundly way past the time she was usually up and about. And in fact she was only just drifting up to a lighter plateau of sleep when the sound of someone tapping at her bedroom door started to penetrate.

By the time she had surfaced enough to open her eyes, however, the person who had been knocking at her bedroom door had opened it and had begun to enter into the room.

She had started to come rapidly awake by the time Brad, with a cup and saucer in his hand, arrived at the side of her bed, and placed what she suspected was a cup of tea upon her bedside table.

She looked from him to the cup of tea and, as she remembered the acrimonious way he had been last night, she struggled to sit up, taking the bedclothes with her.

'What's got into you?' she questioned as she eyed him dubiously.

'I thought it wouldn't come amiss if I did something—nice—for you for a change,' he told her, and, if she could trust it, he seemed to be wearing a genuine smile. And, while her heart felt most peculiarly carefree suddenly that he must be saying that the way she cooked, cleaned and generally kept a weather-eye on him had not gone unnoticed, he was parking himself on the edge of her bed and to her amazement was owning, 'I've been a cantankerous devil, haven't I?'

Mornay looked at him stunned for several wide-eyed moments, and discovered that her voice came out sounding quite husky, when she replied, 'You need to ask?' and felt quite swamped with emotion when he pinned her glance to his and would not let her look away.

'Are you going to forgive me?' he questioned quietly, and all at once Mornay felt all of a tremble inside.

'You haven't been—at all well,' she excused every one of his bad-tempered moments—and the next thing she knew, as her heart suddenly started to flurry wildly, was that he was bending his head, and that his face was coming nearer.

Gently, he saluted her lips with his, and Mornay knew as he drew back that his light kiss had been his way of making up—of making friends. All at once, because she hated to be bad friends with anyone, she just had to smile—her forgiveness complete.

She had thought then that he would get up from her bed and leave her to drink her tea, but as his glance went from her eyes to her smiling mouth he was suddenly still. Then, a kind of groan escaped him, and in the next moment he was reaching for her.

Her heart racing like an express, Mornay had time only to give him a completely unafraid look, and then she was in his arms, and his mouth was once again over hers—only this time his kiss was different.

His mouth was warm and giving, but a hint of growing passion was there that had been entirely absent before, and Mornay, to her surprise, began to experience emotions that caused her to want to meet his passion with her own.

'Brad!' she murmured his name when for a brief moment his lips left hers. Then he was kissing her again, and she was delighting to feel through the thin cotton of her nightdress the strong manliness of his arms.

She delighted even more when, as his mouth left hers and he traced tender kisses down the slender column of her throat, so his hands warmly caressed her back.

'Mornay!' It was he this time who murmured her name, and, as his lips once more took hers, so his hands caressed to her shoulders. Slowly then he began to slide the cap sleeves of her nightdress down her arms.

Mornay felt her cheeks begin to flame. But a fire had started to burn in her for him, and even though she knew that once he had slipped her arms out from her sleeves the low front of her nightdress would drop lower, and that her breasts would be naked, she did not back away.

She wanted him, and as he started to pull back from the passionate kiss they shared she knew that he wanted her. She knew, as he moved the sleeves of her nightdress lower down her arms, that her face was a warm crimson.

But then, while her heart was pounding furiously against her ribs, Brad looked passionately into her eyes and then at her normally creamy complexioned skin, and abruptly she felt all movement in him suddenly cease. The hands that, in caressing movements, had been on the way to leaving her front uncovered, were suddenly still, clamped hard on the material of the cap sleeves of her nightdress and her upper arms.

Then, 'Hell!' he muttered throatily. Then, the sound clearer, though still with that husky male sound, 'I didn't mean this to happen, Mornay, believe me,' he said.

'I . . .' she murmured chokily and, accepting that what had just happened had been as entirely spontaneous for him as it had been for her, she fought desperately hard to rise over what had just been the most earth-shattering emotional experience of her life. Never had she been stirred to want any man before! 'Perhaps,' she found a light note from some amazing somewhere, 'perhaps— Mr Adams—you'd better go.'

She thought she saw a look come to his eyes that seemed to be admiring of the way she was trying to treat the matter lightly. But, as he pushed the sleeves of her nightdress up on to her shoulders and then glanced down to check his handiwork, so Mornay looked down too, and saw, as he must have done, the way the hardened tips of her breasts were peaking against the thin cotton of her nightdress.

Abruptly, he stood up. 'Perhaps—Mrs Adams,' he murmured in a light tone, although Mornay wasn't sure that there was not an undertone of strain there, 'you're right.'

He did not stay after that, but went quickly from her room, leaving Mornay staring after him. Five minutes ticked by and she was still staring—had that been her? Had that warm, feeling, vibrant woman really been her? She had not known that she was capable of such intense, passionate feeling.

CHAPTER SEVEN

THE memory of the way she had been with Brad accompanied Mornay as she bathed and dressed and returned to her room. She was still thinking—had that really been her, had it really happened?—when her glance caught sight of the cup of tea which Brad had brought to her.

Oh, yes, it had happened, she thought, and somehow she felt that she would never again be the person she had been before. Leaving her room, she was in a state of confusion and shyness as she went up the hall, and she had no idea of how she was going to greet Brad when she saw him again.

That problem, however, was solved for her when, as she reached the open sitting-room door, she saw him, standing with his back to her. He was on the telephone, she observed, and she was about to walk on when suddenly she was transfixed to the spot. For quite plainly she heard his clear, clean unaccented tones state, 'She likes roses—send her two dozen with the message "I'll see you soon".'

His call was finished, but he had not so much as put the phone back on its receiver before Mornay was being assaulted by a pain so dreadful it was almost physical. She knew Brad wasn't sending *her* roses—why should he?—and anyway he had no idea whether she liked them or whether she didn't. And the message could hardly apply either, could it, since they were both living in the same property?

Rocked to her foundations by another new emotion which had that morning surfaced in her, Mornay was not certain that she would not have crumpled under the

113

weight of it when, to her undying gratitude, great face-saving quantities of pride arrived.

The phone went down. Brad turned and spotted the blonde-haired woman who was eyeing him coolly. 'How——?' he began, but she was already coldly cutting him off.

'If we don't have breakfast now,' said she who felt she could not swallow so much as a crumb, 'it'll be time for lunch.'

With that Mornay marched on to the kitchen, where she set the kettle to boil and put bread in the toaster while most of her energies were engaged in keeping her thoughts at bay. Yet she was aware of Brad the very moment he entered the kitchen—even though she did not look up.

'Can I help?' he enquired levelly, and she knew then—if she hadn't known it before—that he didn't give a damn about her, or her emotions, and never would.

She shook her head and while keeping her expression entirely indifferent, she made a pot of coffee and put the toast in the toast rack. He carried the coffee-pot to the table while she carried the toast, but though they had shared many meals without a word being said on previous occasions, the silence at this mealtime grew into an unbearable strain for Mornay.

Not that she let it show; she'd have died sooner. Though she was to discover, as Brad sat aloofly opposite her, that he wasn't even aware of the taut, stretched silence. There was nothing strained in his manner anyhow when, obviously not aware that there was any silence to break, he finished the last of his coffee, and casually asked, 'May I borrow your car?'

Biting back an angry retort to the effect that there might be just enough petrol in it to take him a yard past the cliff-edge at Beachy Head, Mornay hid her hurt at his first indication since they'd left Reefingham that he wanted to do something without her. She raised cool eyes—to find that he was regarding her equally coolly.

'You expect me to be here when you get back?' she asked with lofty acid, and knew that neither her comment, nor her arrogance were being kindly received when his eyes narrowed.

'You were thinking of going somewhere?' he challenged icily, and, before she could form a reply, 'With the evidence I have on you—I doubt it,' he rapped, and got up from the table.

Mornay got up from the table too, feeling defeated in more ways than one. She could have saved her breath—she wasn't leaving—she dared not, and he knew it. She went to her bag and extracted her car keys.

'Don't hurry back!' she said sweetly, only she knowing how much that sweet tone had cost her as she placed the keys on the worktop. She turned her back on him, the sound of the outer door opening and closing telling her that he was in a hurry to be away.

She moved to the sitting-room doorway and, standing where she could not be seen, she watched as he drove off down the road. She went back to the kitchen. She was glad he was gone—she hurt, and she wanted to be alone.

So this, she mused dully, was what being in love felt like. Collapsing on to a chair, Mornay was as staggered by her new-found knowledge as she was by the riot of emotions that had raged through her from almost the first moment of opening her eyes that morning.

Though, as she thought about it, she realised that the love which she now acknowledged for Brad Kendrick had been coming on for some time. Her head had been filled with thoughts of him since that very first moment she had seen him. That, of course, was not so surprising in the circumstance of her involvement in his accident, but she doubted that she would have thought so constantly about him had he not had that particular magnetism for her.

This—this love she felt for him was at the base of why he had the power to hurt her. This love she had for him was the reason why she had so recently experienced that emotion, jealousy.

She wanted to believe that she didn't give a hoot whom he sent roses to—but she did. She wanted to believe that she didn't give a light where he had gone to—in her car!—but she did.

Damn him, she thought, and loved him. This, she now plainly saw, was why he had been able to arouse the response he had aroused in her that morning! Never in her life before had she ever experienced such wild, wanting emotions. Lord knew what would or would not have happened had he not called a halt to their love-making. She had little conviction that she would have put up any resistance—and that was before she had actually been aware that she loved him.

Which, she realised, made it imperative—now that she did know that she was in love with him—that she re-sisted with all she had. Not that he was likely to take her in his arms again. Indeed, from the frosty way they had *not* said goodbye just now it wouldn't surprise her if they never so much as spoke to each other again while they remained in Kilcaber.

Mornay got up from her chair and, thinking that she had herself together again and that Brad was never likely to gain so much as a whiff of an idea that she cared for him, she began to collect up the used dishes prior to doing the washing-up when she was stopped dead in her tracks as something suddenly struck her. She had gone to her room last night and had left the washing-up undone, yet there was not a sign of even one of the various saucepans she had used.

Swiftly she left the kitchen and went to the dining-room. She opened the door and, looking in, she leant against the woodwork—there was not a sign of a used pudding plate or anything to be seen.

Weak tears came to her eyes that Brad, who although improved still wasn't fully recovered, had cleared the table and taken all the used china and cutlery out to the kitchen. 'Oh, Brad!' she whispered softly, for, though kitchens and washing-up were all alien to him, he had washed, dried and put away the dishes, leaving everywhere immaculate.

A few moments later Mornay realised that, while she and Brad stayed antagonistic towards each other, he was more likely to think that she hated him than loved him, and that she was going to have to watch those moments when he did something unexpected and kind.

She half wished that she was back in Reefingham when, with her time with him over, and her pride still intact, he would never know... Abruptly her thinking came to a full stop. But only to start up again.

Grief! She had been so engrossed, so taken up with the astonishment of discovering that she was in love with Brad that she had forgotten entirely that with him out of the way she was free to make that urgent telephone call to her brother-in-law.

Wondering at the time she had wasted in getting to the telephone, Mornay hurried to the sitting-room—Brad might come back at any moment. Swiftly she picked up the phone and dialled the Penny Dale number, hoping against hope that it would be Gerry who answered. She didn't want to lie to Claudia, and realised that she was going to have to pretend that she was still in Solihull if luck was against her and her sister picked up the phone.

'Hello.' It was her brother-in-law.

'Hello, Gerry, it's Mornay,' she told him quickly, 'I...'

'Hello,' he greeted her cheerfully, 'we were beginning to think we were never going to hear from you again. How's your mother?'

'Is Claudia there?' Mornay asked urgently.

'She's upstairs seeing to Luke—hang on, I'll give her a shout.'

'No!' Mornay rapidly stopped him, and hurriedly asked, 'Are you still there?'

'Yes,' he replied to her relief, and, seeming to twig that she was a bit agitated about something, 'What's to do, Mornay?'

'I only asked about Claudia because I didn't know whether she was in the same room as you or not, but first—are the police still...?'

'Everything's gone quiet on that front,' Gerry quickly assured her, and Mornay gave a sigh of relief and then went on to break the news of where she was—and who with. Five minutes later, with nothing but, 'You didn't...' and, 'You mean...' and, 'I can't credit it, Mornay,' coming from her brother-in-law, Mornay had told him most of what there was to know.

'The thing is,' she went on, 'that I just don't know when I'll be able to come back. Brad—Kendrick,' she added, 'intimated it would be a month, and...'

'He's treating you all right, Mornay?' her brother-in-law forgot his own panic for a moment to enquire. 'I mean, he's not—er—making you do anything you—er—don't want to do——'

'No,' she quickly assured him, 'apart, that is, from making me stay here to look after him until he's fully recovered. As soon as he's completely well again, I'll be able to return to Reefingham, but meantime I go into a cold sweat whenever I think of Claudia ringing my mother and Mother telling her that she's got a perfectly sound wrist.'

'I'll cover for you there,' Gerry said promptly.

'Can you cover if Robert Naylor rings too?' she queried. 'I've been more than half afraid that he'll ring my mother too, and——'

'Don't worry about it any more, there's a love,' he quickly comforted her. 'I'm only sorry that through me you've been through what you have—even if I do think you were quite nutty to go anywhere near the accident wing of Reefingham General. I'll sort things out this end,' he told her. 'You just keep that man up there until he's fit enough to want to be driven back to London.' Mornay forbore to tell him that Brad's own car was at present being housed at the Belvedere Hotel, Reefingham and was about to ring off when, a little less comfortingly, Gerry was saying, 'You'd better give me your phone number in case I need to get in touch with you.'

'I'd rather you didn't—it's not easy for me to talk . . .'

'I'll not ring you unless it's absolutely essential,' Gerry promised, and Mornay read him the number off the telephone dial.

Having made what she had considered quite an essential phone call herself, and all before Brad had returned, Mornay went to the kitchen and got started on the chores. Again and again, though, as she washed and dried dishes, she could not deny a compulsion to keep glancing out of the window to look for Brad's return.

He was much on her mind as she wiped work surfaces and then swept and mopped the kitchen floor. When the kitchen was back to being presentable, however, and with Brad nowhere to be seen though still to the forefront of her mind, she tried to pin her thoughts on something else.

Should she ring Mr Probert, she wondered, and tell him that she wouldn't be back next week? She ought to, she mused. If by chance she and Brad did leave Kilcaber and she was able after all to go to work next week, then she could always say that her mother's wrist had improved dramatically.

Mornay thought seriously about it for a few minutes and then decided that, since Brad might come back at any moment, and it might be an age before she had another opportunity to make free with the telephone, she would ring Mr Probert. As ever, he was kind, and sent his best wishes to her mother, and Mornay came off the phone a little crimson-cheeked—this time because she hated lies of any sort and had just spent a couple of minutes in evading the truth.

Then she decided that she might as well be hung for a sheep as a lamb, and, with a view to preventing Robert Naylor from inadvertently stirring everything up, she rang his place of work. To her relief, however, she was not called upon to tell any more lies. For, 'Mr Naylor's been trying to contact you,' Vicky, who worked in the stock department of his head office, told her, and went on to say that a decision at higher management level had been made to update their stock-records procedure. 'Which means that everyone, Mr Naylor included, will be working flat out to get everything stock-taken ready to enter on the new system,' Vicky explained. 'I know it's inconvenient, but it looks as though quite a few of them will be working weekends too. Is there any message I can give to him when he rings through?'

Mornay rang off having left no message other than to tell him that she had rung, but felt it couldn't be more convenient as far as she was concerned that the powers-that-be in his firm had taken a decision to restructure their stock procedure. At least it took one worry away from her.

Her anxieties were plenty, however, when lunchtime came and went, but Brad did not. By four o'clock, when he had still not appeared, she had undergone a whole range of emotions that went through fear that he might have had an accident and worry that he might have come over unwell. She then grew angry with herself that she could be so stupid, then angry with him that he hadn't said what time he'd be back. And when she was not in turmoil over him in general, she was beset by jealousy in particular. Damn him, him of the 'send her two dozen roses', and damn his 'I'll see you soon' messages too. The way things were going, she of the two dozen roses fame would see him before she of the Kilcaber prison infamy.

By nine o'clock that evening, however, Mornay's anger and jealousy had departed and she was close to tears in her anxiety about him. She was almost certain then either that he'd been involved in an accident or that his health had suffered a sudden set-back.

At half-past nine she was torn between ringing the hospitals thereabouts and ringing the police, when suddenly the sound which her ears had been straining to hear for most of that day started to appear faintly. When the sound grew louder and she then definitely heard a car pulling up, Mornay was in a highly emotional state, too scared to go and see if it was Brad, in case it was the police who had somehow found out where he was staying, and had come to tell her some dreadful news. Loving, she realised, was hell.

She was hovering in the hallway when, half expecting there to be a ring at the front door, she heard the sound of the rear door into the kitchen being opened. Weak tears of relief sprang to her eyes that it was Brad. Then, even while she conquered her tears, she was suddenly furious with him.

'Where have you been?' she demanded, charging into the kitchen. She wanted more than anything to box his ears that he could so casually stand there, and without a mark on him, while she had been in the throes of a mental breakdown for the past eight or so hours.

She saw his right eyebrow shoot aloft at her demanding manner. But though she fully expected him to take exception to it he was, perhaps because he could see that she was exceedingly het up about something, by contrast extremely calm.

For all that, however, he did not answer her question but, like a conjurer bringing a rabbit out of a hat, he brought his right hand from behind his back and handed her the most beautiful bouquet of roses. 'For you,' he told her, and gently smiled.

Mornay was not one bit mollified. 'You give roses to every female of your acquaintance?' she snapped, knowing full well exactly where his roses were going—in the bin. In the meantime, she placed them down on the worktop.

But Brad, even as an alert light entered his eyes and he carefully scrutinised her expression, was shaking his head. Mornay was well on the way to realising that she had better calm down and fast if she didn't want to give herself away when, with his eyes still quietly on her, he murmured, 'Only to my best girls.'

But whatever he meant by that, Mornay was rapidly coming down from her initial 'hitting the roof' reaction to seeing him casual and unharmed after all the mental agony she had been through that day. So, 'Huh!' she muttered, and left him to sort out what she meant by that while she quickly endeavoured to cancel out any glimmer of a notion he might have received from her outburst that she felt anything at all out of the way for him. 'You weren't looking so well when you left,' she lied without a qualm. 'I couldn't help being worried that you might have collapsed behind the steering-wheel.'

She saw a warm look enter his eyes, and her heart somersaulted when, 'You were worried about me?' he gently asked, and, just as gently, he reached for her and gathered her in his arms.

'S-surely it's only natural I should worry?' she tried to get her head together to tell him. 'What sort of human being would I be not to worry when I know how recently you've been in hospital, and how you're even now still convalescing?'

'I think you're a rather sensitive kind of human,' Brad told her softly, and, looking down into her eyes, he quietly added, 'Perhaps I should have told you that I was going to Perth to pay my mother a visit.'

'Your mother lives in Perth?' Mornay questioned, realising that Perth wasn't too far away. 'You've been to see her?' she asked, not waiting for him to answer her first question. But, with his arms still about her, she realised that she in all probability wasn't thinking straight, and it seemed to her that it was most likely that he was an even bigger liar than she was. 'And if I believe that I'll believe anything,' she remarked tartly.

'You—care?' Brad questioned, but Mornay was certain that there was mockery in his tones. Although in any case, the fact that she did very truly care was the last thing he was going to hear her admit.

'You must have shaken your brains up in that accident!' she scorned, and might have said more on the same theme, only just then Brad took the opportunity of having her in his arms to silence her by placing his mouth over hers.

He did indeed silence her. Or at least, as he broke his gentle kiss and pulled his head back from hers, Mornay was so all over the place that she could not remember a word of what she had been saying.

What she did know, however, was an instinctive feeling that she should not be responding to him for some reason. By luck, as she flicked her glance away from him, her eyes fell on the roses he had brought her.

'I'd—better put these flowers in water,' she told him as she eased herself out of his arms. She had hunted up a vase and filled it with water, and was arranging the roses to their most attractive advantage, when it suddenly dawned on her that she seemed to have changed her mind about throwing them in the bin.

Brad's kiss when he'd taken her in his arms proved to be an isolated incident. Thursday and Friday came and went and the weekend passed in an unruffled kind of way. By Monday Mornay had fully recovered her equilibrium and even if she was still being battered by emotions, all connected with her love for him, then she was swiftly learning how to cope without letting it show.

She sometimes had a feeling that his eyes were on her, but when, casually, she would glance over at him, he was either looking nowhere near her vicinity, or, more often, had his eyes glued to a book, or glued to something of interest outside the window.

They were having breakfast in the kitchen on Tuesday when, again feeling that his glance was on her, Mornay looked quickly across the table at him and discovered that for once she was right.

He didn't seem put out in any way at having been caught staring at her, however—and Mornay later realised that he hadn't been staring at her anyway but more looking her way while he thought his own thoughts, for his manner was quite easy and relaxed as he enquired, 'Isn't it—er—about time we went shopping again?'

Mornay reckoned she knew what his hesitation had been about, too. He was reluctant to go shopping, but recognised that shopping was a necessary evil. This time, however, she had no intention of trying to get to the shops alone—she had made all the phone calls she wanted to make.

'You're a devil for punishment,' she smiled, her smile turning into a laugh when he gave her a pained look, acquiescing to go with her.

She thought it must be over a week now since she had driven her car. Brad had driven it last Wednesday, though, she remembered, and she wondered if she should ask him if he would prefer to drive them to the shops. He, however, unlike her brother-in-law, didn't seem to have any hang-up about being driven by a woman.

With her shopping list complete, Mornay took her car keys from her bag and, leaving Brad to lock up, she went over to her car. Perhaps it was because she'd had Gerry in her mind, and his driving, that as she went round to the driver's side she glanced especially to where he had managed to put a dent in the offside wing. She then had the shock of her life for, fully expecting to see a sizeable dent, she saw instead that there was none!

'It's gone!' she exclaimed in surprise over the top of her car to Brad who had arrived and was ready to get into the passenger seat. 'The dent's gone!'

'Fairies,' he replied.

'You,' she said. 'You had it done! You had it done on Wednesday!' she accused.

'Come round here and say that,' he challenged, and Mornay burst out laughing.

Given all that was happening, all that had happened, and not forgetting that Brad could and probably had spent some time with some female who was not his mother last Wednesday, Mornay felt the happiest she had ever felt in her life as she drove with him to the shops that Tuesday.

There had been absolutely no need for him to have that dent in her car seen to, nor to have it resprayed so that no one would ever know that her car had been in an accident, but he had, and she loved him for it. She realised, of course, that he most likely had a receipt which said something to the effect that there had been a dent there, so that if it ever came to a prosecution he had all the evidence, but she was beginning to think that it would never come to that—not at his instigation, anyhow. And she loved him for that too.

In fact, she loved him so much just then that when she got round to wondering how much longer they were going to stay in Kilcaber she experienced a tremendous pang of regret that it could not be for much longer now. For, although she realised that Brad must still be feeling not one hundred per cent fit yet, outwardly he seemed as if there was nothing wrong with him. She felt she knew, regretfully, that the moment that he did feel one hundred per cent again, he would want to return to London—and that they would part.

It was then that she decided she was going to make the most of her time with him. She felt happy. She wanted to have some happy memories for when that dreadful day dawned that they parted, and she had to accept that their paths would never converge again.

Tuesday went on being a happy day; so, too, did Wednesday. Thursday also was a day when she and Brad got on well without either of them getting cross with the other about anything. On Friday, however, as it was getting on for the time when Mornay usually began to prepare the evening meal, the phone—which had remained silent all the time they had been there—suddenly rang. Mornay made a startled movement from the unexpectedness of it, and Brad smiled at her as he went over to the instrument and, in his firm voice, gave their telephone number.

Mornay realised that someone was taking their time in answering him when, 'Hello?' he queried, and a moment later told her, 'Somebody must have misdialled,' as he replaced the receiver.

She smiled, and said, 'I'll go and make a start in the kitchen.'

She might then have forgotten all about the wrong number call of Friday. But when at around the same time on Saturday the telephone rang, and with the same result—that when Brad answered it in his all-masculine voice no one replied—she began to have edgy thoughts. She hoped it was just her guilty conscience that was making her have such thoughts, but—was Gerry trying to get in touch?

That possibility fidgeted away at Mornay all the next day—and caused her to wonder at her chances of getting in touch with him to see if everything was all right. There was no chance, however, for every time she went anywhere near to the telephone that day Brad seemed to appear.

He was in the sitting-room with her, reading from the pile of Sunday papers they had that morning driven to purchase, when at around six-thirty that evening the phone went again.

Oh, no, Mornay thought worriedly, and became more worried when Brad went to answer it. Her worries rapidly increased when this time, having picked up the phone, Brad said not a word.

It was then that she knew he was suspicious. Two consecutive phone calls when he'd answered the phone only to hear the dialling tone a short while later, followed by a third consecutive phone call at more or less the same time, was enough to make him so, she realised.

She calculated that a full half-minute went by with Brad just standing there, saying nothing, and as her anxiety peaked it was in her mind to call loudly—loud enough for any caller to hear—something along the line of, 'Who is it, Brad?' in an endeavour to warn the caller—if it was Gerry—that it was not she who had picked up the phone.

But the caller, forced by the silence coming from the other end, must, it seemed, have decided to risk a query. Because, before Mornay could call out anything, a grim sort of look was setting on Brad's face, and she heard him grate tersely, 'Who wants her?' She saw Brad's expression go thunderous, then, without comment, he was handing the phone to her.

Mornay took the phone and with a fast-beating heart hoped against hope that Brad would leave her to take her call in private. He did no such thing, but, giving her a look of intense dislike, he turned his back on her and went to look out of the window.

Momentarily, fully aware that his ears would be flapping, Mornay hated him. Then, 'Hello,' she said, and discovered that she had been right to fear that her brother-in-law had been trying to make contact, for as soon as he heard her voice, so she heard his.

'I know it's difficult for you, Mornay, and I know I haven't helped by ringing, but I had to risk it.'

'Is——?'

'Don't say anything but yes or no,' Gerry broke in quickly to stop her before she could say anything that might incriminate him. 'Everything's fine here,' he went on to quickly assure her, 'it's just that Claudia's a bit—er—fretful.'

'Fretful?' Mornay straight away forgot his instructions to query.

'She's not in post-natal depression, or anything like that,' Gerry quickly assured her, 'but Luke's proving more demanding than any of the others were, and she's worrying herself silly about how she's going to cope with the four girls and Luke when I go back to work tomorrow. I've already had an extra week off, so I just have to go in tomorrow,' he told her.

'I—see,' Mornay said slowly.

'The thing is,' he went on, 'with Claudia thinking that you managed to get time off easily enough when your mother needed you for such a simple thing as a sprained wrist, she's got it into her head that you wouldn't hesitate to have another week off to come and give her a hand.'

'I—er—don't see how I can,' Mornay replied, starting to feel wretched as her heart went out to her sister.

'I knew it was a long shot,' Gerry sighed, 'but I felt I just had to ask.'

Mornay put the phone down after the call with her thoughts on how devoted her brother-in-law was to her sister, and how worried he had sounded. Though she was not thinking of anything in particular in the next second, for suddenly Brad, in furious mood, was standing in front of her, and instinctively she knew that there was going to be trouble!

And there was. Before she could so much as draw another breath, 'Who was that?' he snarled threateningly.

It took Mornay all her time not to swallow apprehensively at his foreboding expression, but she hoped she had more spirit than to let him or any man browbeat her, so she snapped hotly, 'I thought you'd asked?' only just remembering in time that the only thing Brad had said down the phone this time had been, 'Who wants her?'

'You told me Robert was your boyfriend's name!' he rapped, clearly not taking kindly to her nerve in answering back.

'So it is!'

'So who's Gerry?' he demanded, and suddenly Mornay was starting to panic.

'Just—a friend,' she replied, knowing, whatever else she did not know, that she must not let him know that Gerry was her brother-in-law.

'How did he know where to contact you?' Brad charged, his mood not getting any sweeter as he pursued his interrogation.

'I rang him,' Mornay told him defiantly, but was able to see then that Brad wasn't so much mad that she had made the call but, valuing his privacy, was incensed that she had risked his 'hideaway' cover. 'I rang him,' she repeated, just to let him know that she wasn't afraid of the fearsome glint that came to his dark eyes, 'on the day you went to visit your ''mother''!' Immediately she wanted those defiant words back, for with an enraged growl Brad took a furious stride forward. 'Don't you dare touch me!' she yelled, fearing she knew not what, but, as her hands went out as though to push him away, knowing with yet more instinct that the time for brave heroics was not now.

'Why the...?' Brad began, but by then he had taken an angry hold of her hands. And then, it was as though the touch of her had inflamed his temper some more. At any rate, there was perhaps half a second when if she'd any sense she had a moment to snatch her hands free and race out of there. But—she didn't.

Because, oddly, when she knew full well that there was the very devil riding on his back, just the touch of Brad's skin, of his hands on hers, was affecting her. Her lovely blue eyes were wide in her face as she stared at him in a stunned kind of a way—and then Brad was pulling her to him.

Half a second later, and she was in his arms. Furiously, he kissed her. With his arms iron bands around her, he pulled her closer to him, moulding her body to his, while he claimed her mouth again and again.

Mornay tried to struggle against him. Quite desperately she attempted to tell herself that this was not right. But, as passion began to rage in her, she started to press her body voluntarily closer to him—and at her response he no longer had to use his superior strength to bind her to him.

'Mornay!' he cried on a ragged sound, holding her to him with one arm as one hand undid the top two buttons on her blouse, and Mornay knew more delight when, bending his head, he traced kisses to the V of the satiny skin he had revealed in the cleavage of her breasts.

Her arms were around him when he moved unhurriedly with her to the settee. 'Oh, Brad,' she moaned his name, and was lost to everything but him when he lay down with her on the settee and caressed her and undid the remaining buttons on her blouse.

She had no idea that her breasts were totally naked until, as one of his hands caressed warmly from her waist, he gently but unexpectedly moved that hand until he had captured that naked, swollen globe.

'Oh!' she gasped, and knew her colour was crimson as, sending her into ecstasies of rapture, Brad moulded that breast tenderly in his hands.

Wanting to feel his body too, she tried to undo his shirt buttons with her trembling fingers, making a hash of it until Brad, suddenly smiling down at her, undid his shirt for her.

She almost said thank you, but by then Brad had come to rest his uncovered, hair-roughened chest over her satiny breasts. And, 'Oh!' she breathed again. For suddenly he wasn't angry any more. Suddenly, all the fury seemed to have gone out of him and he was being gentle with her, and she loved him.

She wasn't sure that she did not call his name again when his mouth left hers and he traced warm, virile kisses down her throat and to her breasts until his lips stayed at one pink, hard peak. Then he was kissing her breasts and moulding her to him again, and one hand left her breasts and moved to the waistband of her skirt.

Mornay knew then that she would deny him nothing. Never had she been in the grip of an emotion such as this, one which knew no holding back.

Or so she thought. Though even afterwards, she was never sure whether she was making a protest or not. But, feeling the need to take a deep breath in all this that was so new, she suddenly placed a nervous staying hand over the one that was already pulling down her zip, and Brad took the opportunity to study her burning face.

What he read there she had no idea, although she felt that he must see that she wanted him, and would not hold back once she had got over her moment of nervousness. But, after staring into her all-giving blue eyes for some tense seconds, suddenly, and to her utter bewilderment, he groaned, 'Oh, my...' and left her and—as if the devil himself were after him—went from the room!

Quite how long she sat staring after him, Mornay could not have said. Nor could she have said how long it took her to come to an awareness that she was half sitting, half lying, partly naked, looking to the door as if hoping he would come back. When that realisation did hit her, however, she moved.

In next to no time she was in her bedroom, properly dressed, with the door firmly closed while she leant against it and tried to get her head back together.

Oh, dear heaven, how was she going to face him again after her wanton display just now? Again she was set to wonder—had that person who had clung to him so passionately been her?

She moved away from the door and for the next hour went through agonies of thinking that she should have fought Brad all the way, while knowing that what she should have done and what she had done were two entirely different things. Her head might initially have put up some resistance, but she had been weakened from that first moment of him taking hold of her hands.

Having gone through agonies, however, Mornay knew that if Brad was not to gain so much as a whisper of how deeply she cared for him, then she was going to have to show him a very different person from the one she had all that week.

No more smiling or laughing at any amusing quip he made, she was in the middle of instructing herself firmly, when, to make her spin round in startled anguish, there came a tap at her door.

Wanting badly not to answer, Mornay knew without thinking about it that Brad would see nothing wrong in coming straight in if she kept him waiting too long. Feeling torn between a desire to hide and a desire to yell at him to go away, Mornay grabbed at what courage she could and went to the door.

Opening the door, she saw him tall, dark and steady-eyed as he studied her face. She knew, even as she renewed her resolution to be cold to him, that her colour was high, but she held his gaze unflinchingly as she waited for him to announce the purpose of his visit—which, when he did, caused her to stare at him some more.

For, 'Dinner's ready,' he announced. All thought of preparing an evening meal had completely passed her by. Oh, Brad, she wanted to murmur softly as it penetrated that, though she was only too well aware that he was practically helpless in the kitchen, he had made a meal for her.

But she did not murmur anything of the kind. From somewhere she was remembering the importance of showing him that he meant less than nothing to her. 'Thank you,' she told him coldly, and, throwing his efforts back in his face, 'but I'm not hungry.' She saw at once from the way any gentleness in his expression suddenly and instantly evaporated that he liked neither her tone nor what she said, so, in case he might get round to thinking that his rejection of her had taken away her appetite for dinner, she added more for good measure. 'In fact,' she tossed in arrogantly, 'I'd like to go back to Reefingham if——' It was as far as she got, for, his expression all at once as black as thunder, Brad was wasting no time in cutting her off.

'Panting for Gerry?' he snarled, and then, very nearly paralysing her with the savagery of his tongue, 'Why bother?' he sneered. 'From your response to me not too long ago, I'd have said any man would have done!'

A shocked gasp left her, then, 'You—swine!' she choked, and had to look away lest he saw the sudden, mortifying tears of hurt that suddenly sprang to her eyes.

Whether he had seen them before she could blink them away, though, Mornay didn't know. But suddenly, as if taken by instant remorse, he groaned, 'Oh, hell!' and in the next moment he had taken her gently in his arms. 'That was a foul thing to say,' he apologised, and sounded sincere. And, as if realising the effect he had on her, 'You're so damned confused you don't know where the hell you're at, do you?' he asked of her quietly.

But as fear hit at her heart she was too agitated to know what he was referring to. Was he merely referring to the state of confusion he must know she was in from their lovemaking—and the response he had awakened in all that was so new to her? Or was he referring to the confusion he might be thinking she was feeling if he guessed at her love for him? Mornay realised that she had better act—and quickly.

Pride rose in her over the joy and comfort she experienced at being in his arms, when, grasping at every ounce of strength, both mental and physical, she pushed him away hard and pulled out of his arms.

'I know where the hell I *want* to be!' she told him furiously—and saw that that hadn't met with his favour either.

She saw his chin jut at an aggressive angle as his arms fell down to his sides. Then he had taken a step back, and she could see his eyes were glinting with ice when he barked, 'Tough!' and walked away.

CHAPTER EIGHT

WHEN, Mornay wondered when she awakened the next morning, had she ever felt happy to be sharing this isolated spot with Brad? She felt far from happy as she left her bed and started to get ready to face the day. Any happiness she had thought she'd known had completely gone.

She returned from getting bathed and dressed, and knew that she still loved Brad with all her being—but she found no joy in that. Thank goodness for pride, she mused dejectedly as she brushed her long blonde hair and tucked it behind her ears prior to going along to the kitchen. Pride, if nothing else, would get her through this day.

'Good morning,' Brad greeted her courteously enough, coming in as she was preparing scrambled eggs on toast.

'Good morning,' she replied in kind, but felt that there was a definite strain in the atmosphere.

She was sure of that strain when not another word passed between them, but a taut silence ensued while she did a collection of other jobs which included taking a freshly made pot of coffee to the table.

In silence she left the scrambled eggs keeping warm while she seated herself at the table. From beneath her long lashes she noted that Brad had followed suit, and she tucked into half a grapefruit with every appearance of having a healthy appetite. Then she left the table to put scrambled egg on freshly buttered toast. She was conscious as she did so that Brad too had left the table. From the corner of her eye she saw him clear their place settings of the dishes they had so far used. He was back in his place at the breakfast table, however, when, without a word, she placed a plate of scrambled eggs on toast in front of him.

Silence reigned, and Mornay was halfway through her scrambled egg when she suddenly realised that she had been so busy with her other thoughts that she had forgotten to remember her usual care about what she placed before Brad. In view of that first breakfast she had given him of scrambled egg when he'd had the utmost difficulty in cutting up his toast, she had been particularly careful not to ever again give him anything on toast.

She took another glance beneath her lashes—at his hands this time—and saw that, as well as coping magnificently, he was holding his knife and fork in a quite normal manner. Indeed, so normal were his actions, there was no sign that there had ever been anything the matter with him.

It was that thought—that there was no sign that there had ever been anything the matter with him—which caused Mornay to raise her eyes to his face. Her heart began to beat a little faster as she took in his normal healthy colour, and the rested look of him. Quite suddenly then, she was ready to swear that he was once again a fit and healthy man.

And for that she was enormously grateful. Though abruptly, as Brad all at once looked up, so Mornay, who had been studying him, found herself caught out. What could she do? For a split second as his dark eyes looked straight into hers she was stumped—which left her only one method of defence available.

Her voice was challenging when, 'You're well again now, aren't you?' she smartly attacked—and saw the angry glint that came to his eyes at her tone.

She was not, therefore, particularly surprised when he retaliated in harsh kind, 'If you mean, have I recovered from the injuries I sustained when you drove your car at me and then, like a coward, drove on without stopping,' he attempted to shoot her down in flames, 'then I've been *fully well* for over a week now!'

His remarks about her cowardice hurt, even if he had got the wrong person. But she was beginning to think that there was little he could say when he was in acid mood that wouldn't hurt. So, tilting her chin an angry fraction, she favoured him with a cool, unsmiling look of her own. 'Then perhaps you wouldn't mind telling me what the blazes I'm doing here looking after you,' she questioned stiffly. 'You don't need me!' she told him for good measure—and was straight away slapped down for her trouble.

'You're being repetitious,' Brad told her curtly, and, while Mornay started to grow indignant at his insinuation that her talk of wanting to return to Reefingham was getting boring, he went on to lay it on the line. 'My good health may have returned, but nothing else has changed.' His voice had taken on a silky edge when, leaning back in his chair, he threatened arrogantly, 'I'm sure I don't have to remind you that the police will still be looking for the low-down hit-and-run type who rendered me unconscious one night last month.'

And at that, something in Mornay snapped. 'It's a pity you ever woke up!' she hissed furiously, and, throwing down her napkin, she was off her chair and halfway out of the kitchen when he mocked,

'I adore you too, sweetheart.'

Mornay spent a lot of time over the next few days wishing that Gerry Overton had never telephoned. So, OK, maybe she had, prior to that call, been in a fool's paradise, thinking that she was happy, but surely that had to be better than what she had now? The atmosphere between her and Brad was more strained than ever. She supposed she should apologise for her 'pity you ever woke up' remark, but he hadn't apologised for his threatening remark which had provoked it, so why the hell should she?

Thursday morning dawned dull and cheerless. Great, Mornay thought—it matched her mood. 'Good morning,' Brad started the day right anyhow as he tossed her a civil greeting when he came into the kitchen.

'Good morning,' Mornay responded coolly in kind, and wondered just how much longer they were going to go on like this. Though Brad didn't seem to be showing any sign that he felt anything to be amiss, and she was darned sure she wasn't going to be the one to suggest that there might be.

As on Tuesday and Wednesday, breakfast was taken in total silence. Mornay munched her way through toast and marmalade that tasted like chaff and knew that the only thing that prevented her from again suggesting that they returned to Reefingham was Brad's acid implication that such a topic of conversation was boring.

She finished her toast and took her plate to the sink. She heard Brad move, but did not turn round. She was aware of him, tautly aware of him standing somewhere behind her, and suddenly her nerve-ends seemed more stretched than ever. Needing some action then as never before, she extended a hand towards the kettle, intending to fill it and set it to boil, but her hand never reached that far. Because, as she pushed out a hand, a long arm came from behind her and, as if yanked by some puppeteer, she jumped back in nervous tension.

Too late, she saw that it had never been in Brad's mind to touch her. Too late, she saw that he had merely been reaching for a teaspoon which was by the side of the kettle, and which she had missed putting in his coffee-saucer. Too late, she saw, as he must have done, that the way she had jumped back from him must have seemed as though she was afraid he was going to take her in his arms.

'Oh, for lord's sake!' she heard him grunt grimly, and the next sound she heard was the sound of him slamming short-temperedly out of the bungalow.

He had never done that before, and it upset Mornay. It was clear that he was upset too, but it was too late then to wish that she'd had more control of her reflexes. She hadn't meant to jump back like that, but she knew that there was no way she was going to explain that her unguarded reaction had been brought about by the uneasy tension between them.

Ten minutes later, with no sign of Brad returning, Mornay was starting to rebel and wonder why she should want to explain anything anyhow. If he'd asked for a spoon she'd have passed one over to him. No wonder she'd jumped. It served him right for coming creeping up behind her. Perhaps he'd be more careful in future.

Thoughts of the future brought to mind thoughts of a return to Reefingham, which in turn brought a reminder of Penny Dale and her sister and her family.

As on the only other occasion when Brad had left her in the bungalow on her own, Mornay wondered at the time she had wasted in getting to the telephone. This time, though, as she went to the sitting-room Mornay knew an odd reluctance to dial that number in Penny Dale, though why, she had no idea. She still loved her sister as much as always, and as always she wanted to help her—if she could.

The words 'if she could' played back in her mind as she dialled. Claudia wanted her to go and stay with her to give her a bit of help with the children, but how could she? Mornay didn't even know why she was ringing Claudia, though as she waited she supposed it must be something to do with the bond of love that had been forged in their growing years.

'Mornay!' her sister gave a glad cry when she heard her voice. 'Oh, I knew you wouldn't let me down—how soon can you get here?'

'Er—I'm not in Reefingham,' Mornay thought she had better explain.

'You're not still away with the parents!' Claudia exclaimed. 'Good heavens!' she went on. 'I could hardly believe it when Gerry said that because of Mother's wrist you were going on holiday with them. Although,' she conceded, 'you being you, perhaps I can. Anyhow,' she went rushing on, 'Mother's had you for long enough now, so you just tell her you're coming to me and——'

'But—er—my job!' Mornay cut in, clutching at straws and still trying to keep the truth—the truth that would threaten Claudia's security—from her.

'Oh, Mr Probert's an old softee; if you've used up all your holiday allowance he'll give you some more time off, I'm certain. Especially when you tell him how much you're needed here.'

From clear memory, it seemed to Mornay that there always had been a certain amount of pandemonium in her sister's happy home, but, 'Are things really that bad?' she gently asked.

'Chaotic is an understatement!' Claudia replied, and to Mornay's horror she was sure she heard a catch in her sister's voice as she told her shakily, 'Luke never stops crying from morning to night, the house is a tip and Gerry's had to work late the last three nights to compensate for having all of last week off. I'm telling you, Mornay,' she went on, and there was a definite break in her voice, 'I t-tell you I'm getting so depressed, I-I just can't cope!'

Mornay stayed trying to calm her for another five minutes. Then a tearful Claudia was telling her she'd have to go, that baby Luke was screaming his lungs off, and begging her to come and give her some help.

'I'll see what I can do,' was the best Mornay could promise, but she came away from the telephone feeling exceedingly worried. In normal circumstances she'd have been over at Penny Dale like a shot.

But, she sighed as she returned to the kitchen and got busy with the chores, these were not normal circumstances. Nor, though, was it normal for Claudia to be depressed, and Mornay found that very worrying.

Having finished in the kitchen, she went to the sitting-room with a duster and fretted that, when Claudia had always been there when she had needed her, she should be letting her down at this time. Not that she could recall ever having any major problem that she hadn't been able to work through for herself, but it pained Mornay that the best she could tell her sister was 'I'll see what I can do'.

She was entirely forgetful, as her concern increased, that, far from letting her sister down, she was in fact, by being so many miles away from Penny Dale, doing what she had to to ensure the future security of her sister and her sister's offspring.

Her anxieties, though, had reached a climax by the time she heard Brad return. Immediately she wanted to go to him and plead for him to let her return to Reefingham, but she was still smarting from the 'boring' label he had given the subject.

She guessed, however, that her anxiety must have been showing when, a minute or so later, he stepped into the sitting-room, took one look at her and instantly frowned. Then, flicking her an annoyed look, he turned abruptly about and, as if he thought himself the cause of her anxiety, he showed her just how much he wanted to touch her again—by striding out again.

But, 'Brad!' she called urgently, as she swallowed on the realisation that any passing desire he might have had for her was just that—passing. She saw him halt by the door, and saw him slowly turn, and she fought frantically for something to say that would not give away any of what had to be kept most secret from him.

'Well?' he barked when, instead of telling him why she had called his name, she continued to stand there looking huge-eyed and worried.

'I . . .' Mornay began, and then, finding her powers of invention were suddenly in hiding, 'My sister wants to see me!' she blurted out in one go.

'Your—sister wants to see you?' he questioned, one eyebrow raising aloft as he took a couple of casual steps back into the room.

'I rang her while you were out,' she confessed, and was made to suffer another dark look for her deceit in using the phone only when his back was turned.

But, 'Naturally,' was his only comment, sarcastic though that one word was.

'The thing is,' Mornay continued slowly, feeling her way as she went, 'my sister—well, she's a bit depressed, and—and I think it would cheer her up if I—if we—she and I,' she pressed on, starting to flounder at his look that said he thought she was lying about the whole of it, 'if we could see——' She broke off when his look became totally sceptical. 'She *is* depressed!' she snapped, starting to get angry. 'You didn't hear her . . .'

'What's she depressed about?' Brad questioned her toughly, and Mornay glared at him.

'If you must know,' she flared, 'she had a baby—some while ago,' she tacked on hastily, and backtracked over what she had just told him, but could see nothing in what she had said that would link Gerry in as being the driver of her car that particular night. 'Some women can feel low for ages afterwards,' she enlightened him for extra emphasis, even though she was fully aware that Claudia's problem was not one of a hormonal imbalance, but the fact of Luke's being more demanding than his sisters, and that of Claudia's finding difficulty in getting into a routine.

'She doesn't get on with your mother?'

Brad's bald statement caused Mornay to stare at him in some surprise. How on earth had he known that? She was sure she hadn't said... 'No,' she confirmed, 'that is—what's whether she gets on with my mother got to do with anything?' she flared.

'You tell me!' he grunted. 'It seemed to me an obvious question since, according to what you've told me, your sister lives with your parents. I could only assume, with your sister wanting to see you, that things can't be too amicable in the Solihull household.'

'Oh,' Mornay murmured, and, fully aware that a pair of dark eyes were firmly fixed on her creamy complexion which, as heat washed over her, she was sure had turned to a 'found out' pink, 'Er—Claudia—er—doesn't live in Solihull—er—actually,' she was made to confess.

'She doesn't?' he questioned, a grim light starting to enter his eyes.

Grief, thought Mornay, hoping, since it seemed that he took great exception to being told lies, that this was the last lie he ever found out about. 'I never actually said that she did,' she told him, but could see he had awarded her no merit marks for pointing that out.

'Where—*actually*—does she live?' he questioned.

'With her husband—and five children,' Mornay stalled.

'Surely not in a shoe,' he commented drily, and Mornay was suddenly struck by a feeling of wanting to laugh.

Nerves rather than amusement were the cause for that, she quickly decided, and as quickly realised too that in trying to avoid telling him what it seemed he was determined to know, she was drawing greater attention to her reluctance—which was only going to make him wonder his famous 'Why?'.

'She lives in a house, as a matter of fact,' she told him, 'in Penny Dale,' and since if he'd never heard of

Penny Dale it wouldn't take him long to find out where it was, 'It's near Reefingham,' she told him.

'How near?'

Damn you, Mornay fumed, feeling suddenly irritated with him and his mind that left no question unasked. 'About five miles,' she shrugged, as though carelessly.

'On your doorstep, in fact,' Brad commented.

'If you like,' she said coldly, and weathered his long, level look which told her as clearly as if he'd said it that he was remembering the morning they had left Reefingham and how the only person she had telephoned had been her employer.

Mornay half expected some acid comment from him to the effect that it would not have surprised him had she told him that she and her sister didn't get on either, since she had gone away without a word despite their living on each other's doorstep. Or, she thought, perhaps some acid comment on the lines of being surprised that her sister wanted to see her when, apart from living near to each other, they did not otherwise appear to be close at all.

But, whatever Mornay expected, it was she who was surprised when, taking her back to that morning three weeks ago, he suddenly and abruptly clipped, 'Are you packed?'

'Packed?' she questioned witlessly.

'If we're to make Penny Dale before nightfall, we'd better get started,' he replied loftily.

There was more to be done than pack their belongings, however. But, in less time than she would have thought, the beds—at her instigation—had been stripped, and Mrs Macdonald, the woman who had greeted them on their arrival, had been contacted and asked if she would mind coming to clear out the cupboards. Then, with Brad doing the driving this time, and stopping at Mrs Macdonald's home to drop off the key,

they were heading back the way which three weeks ago
they had come.

As an aching pang of regret took Mornay, she was
glad that Brad had opted to drive. It seemed odd, when
she had known joy and sadness, happiness and dejection,
that she should feel such regret at having left that
bungalow in Kilcaber. But, now that she knew that her
time with Brad Kendrick was at an end, regret, a very
real regret, was what she felt.

She knew full well that she should be glad he had
shown himself to have a heart when she had told him
of her sister's depression, for, as he once had before, he
could have easily answered 'Tough'. But, he hadn't, and
she loved him, and after today she was never going to
see him again and—she wanted the journey never to end.

'Are you hungry?' Brad suddenly enquired, and
Mornay had to quickly choke down weak tears that were
at that moment threatening.

'A bit,' she lied, and realised as they stopped for lunch
that what she was doing, even while part of her knew
that she should be hurrying to get to Claudia, was trying
to delay the hour when she must say a final farewell to
the man who held her heart.

Once lunch was over Brad drove for a further three
hours without stopping. By then Mornay thought that
she had got herself more under control so that, had he
asked whether she would like to stop for tea, she would
have told him no.

But he did not ask, and, perversely, she started to
worry that he might need a rest. 'Shall we stop for a cup
of tea?' she asked, and as he pulled in at a service area
she could only wonder at the contrary person she had
become since love had fired its blunderbuss of varying
emotions at her.

They did not spend long over their tea, but when, still
thinking that he might appreciate a rest, she suggested
that she would drive, he would not hear of it. 'It's not

far now,' he told her evenly. It was about that time that Mornay awakened to a sense of danger.

They were on their way again when, racking her brains, she felt certain that, when asking if she was packed, Brad had then followed up with—not 'If we're to make Reefingham before nightfall . . .' but, 'If we're to make Penny Dale'!

Penny Dale! she thought alarmed, and at the thought that he intended to drive her to her sister's home her alarm started to turn to panic. She couldn't let him drive her to Claudia's, she just couldn't! If Gerry wasn't working late and, having worked late three nights on the trot she thought that there was a fair chance he might finish work on time or even early that night, then he could well be there by the time she and Brad drove up.

With her head swimming with endless complications which might conceivably ensue, Mornay felt too het up to leave it to see whether Brad took the Penny Dale turn before she said anything.

'Er——' she said in a strangled kind of way, and then, plunging straight in, 'We—er—should have rung the Belvedere to let them know you were coming to pick up your car tonight.'

'I don't suppose they'll have parted with it,' he replied evenly, which, frustratingly, told her absolutely nothing about his intentions once they reached the borders of her home town.

'I don't suppose they will,' she agreed carefully, and left it a moment or two before she added casually, 'Will you be driving back to London tonight, do you think?'

'I hadn't given it any thought,' he annoyingly let fall.

Then damn well give it some thought, she wanted to yell at him, but didn't. For the next ten minutes her thoughts were taken up with knowing that it was out of the question for him to take her to Penny Dale, while at the same time she wondered how the dickens she was going to stop him if he was decided upon doing just that—and, how in creation was she going to handle it if she couldn't stop him?

The sign said 'Reefingham,' and they went by it with Mornay racking her brains while her stomach churned within her. Then 'Penny Dale 5 miles', said a sign, and as, to her horror, Brad steered the car in that direction, she broke into speech.

'There's no need for you to drive out of your way!' she told him urgently. 'Th——'

'It's no bother,' Brad told her easily. 'After the miles we've come today, another five miles is neither here nor there.'

'Yes, but—but, you must want to get to the Belvedere to reclaim your car and...' Her voice petered out when he gave her a sideways, eyebrow-raised look. 'You've been so good already,' she hopped hastily on to another tack. 'It doesn't seem fair that you should...' Her voice faltered when, as he flicked her another all-seeing glance, she realised he must have seen that she was in a stew about something.

'You've said many things during our time together,' he murmured sardonically, 'but never, Mornay, have you accused me of being "good".'

Go to hell, she wanted to tell him, but instead, she sighed defeatedly, and told him ungraciously, 'I shall only have to leave Claudia to run you back.'

'I wouldn't dream of permitting it,' Brad answered suavely. 'I'm sure the local taxi service will be more than adequate.'

Apart from giving him directions to her sister's home, Mornay had not another word to say to him. In relative silence she fumed for the rest of the way, and put her faith in Gerry's not being home from work yet, in Brad's not staying for longer than it took to summon a taxi, and in everything's turning out all right.

Fate, Mornay soon realised, was laughing up her sleeve. For from the very start everything began to turn

out all wrong. From the instant Brad pulled up outside
Claudia's home and Mornay saw that her sister was in
the garden taking advantage of the sun's rays that late
Thursday afternoon, one tearing-apart emotion after
another flooded through Mornay.

'Mornay!' Claudia cried in delight as, with Brad following, Mornay went over the path and on to the lawn,
and Claudia came over to greet them.

Hugging her sister, Mornay was pleased to see that
she was looking far more cheerful than she had feared
she might. Though, knowing something of her sister's
character, it was highly probable that she was putting
up a show in front of the stranger she had brought with
her.

Which reminded Mornay—not that she could have
forgotten him. 'Claudia,' she smiled, and turning to the
tall, dark, watchful-eyed man standing silently by her
side, 'this is Brad Kendrick,' she introduced him, hoping
against hope that Claudia had been so taken up with her
family that she had not chanced to hear his name mentioned anywhere in connection with an accident in
Reefingham's High Street. 'Brad,' she continued smile,
'this is my sister, Claudia Overton.'

As soon as her sister's surname had left her lips,
Mornay was wishing it hadn't. Far better, she thought,
as the two shook hands, not to feed him any information which he didn't absolutely have to know; was it
too soon for her to make noises about ringing for a taxi?

'Where are the girls?' she questioned, guessing that
perhaps Gerry's mother must have taken them for an
hour to give Claudia a break, and again wished that she
had not said something when she heard Claudia's reply.

'Gerry's taken them for ice-creams,' she announced
sunnily, and as Mornay caught the look in Brad's eyes
that plainly told her that Gerry's name had registered,
'Gerry's my husband,' Claudia smilingly explained, 'and
the girls are my four daughters. And this,' she said

proudly, leading the way to the pram which was situated close to where she had been sitting, 'is my son.'

Luke was beautiful, and at any other time Mornay would have peered into the pram and have crooned over the little mite. But her nerves were starting to feel stretched to breaking-point, and all she had in mind to do just then was to get Brad away from Penny Dale before Gerry returned. She doubted very much that Gerry would give anything away, but just the two being introduced to each other represented a risk, and yet more complications.

She was making a show of admiring the sound-asleep babe just the same when, to make her heart sink, she heard Claudia offer Brad some sort of refreshment. At any other time she would have been surprised had Claudia not done so, but this time she could have wished that her sister had forgotten her good manners.

'Brad isn't staying!' she found herself hastily refusing for him, and when she glanced from her sister to a pair of dark, all-seeing, all-thinking eyes, 'You said something about taking a taxi back, didn't you?' she queried, forcing a smile.

'So I did,' he replied levelly. 'Perhaps . . .' he hinted.

'May I use your phone to ring Ibbotson's taxis?' Mornay asked, starting to feel a trace of relief that it wouldn't be much longer now before Brad went.

'Of course,' Claudia replied, and added with a smile, 'they're all male drivers on that firm.' Then, before Mornay had taken a footstep in the direction of the telephone, she promptly sent any trace of relief flying, and very nearly caused her heart-failure, when by way of explanation for her last remark, 'I noticed when you arrived that you were doing the driving,' she addressed Brad. And brightly she went on to suggest, 'Perhaps you, like my husband, can't abide to be driven anywhere by a woman.'

An almost soundless cry, half strangled at birth left Mornay, who was unable to prevent it. Unfortunately, one of the two people standing near picked it up. It was the one person she would have preferred not to have heard. Because suddenly Brad had pinned her gaze with his, and dark eyes were looking straight into panicking blue ones.

She knew at once that he had sensed that there was something amiss, and she panicked some more when she saw an alert, considering look enter his eyes. She had seen that alert look before and she knew, where Claudia didn't, that Brad Kendrick had been born asking, 'Why?', and that he was about to start asking questions any minute now.

Rooted to the spot, all thoughts of going to ring for a taxi forgotten, Mornay tried to get in first to say something, anything to detract him from his purpose. But her throat was dry and nothing would come, and anyway, Brad had got in first.

'Mornay never mentioned that your husband shares my aversion,' he smiled, full of charm, to Claudia.

Don't! Don't answer him! Mornay wanted to shriek, knowing full well that he had no such aversion. But her sister was taking the man she had brought to her home on face-value, and was responding warmly to his charm, and did answer—openly. 'I'm not surprised,' she smiled back at him. 'Mornay's probably still peeved at him over the last time he asked her to hand over her car keys.'

'No!' Mornay tried to get in, but her sister merely took it that she was denying that she was still peeved with Gerry, and hardly needed the invitation Brad gave her to continue.

'What happened?' he seemed pleasantly interested to know, and, while Mornay was striving to control her panic by telling herself that Claudia couldn't tell him anything because Gerry wouldn't have told her about the accident, Claudia blithely continued.

'I was in hospital at the time, having Luke,' she said, glancing to the babe in the pram. 'Both Gerry and Mornay were coming to see me when Gerry's car went on the blink, so Gerry rang Mornay to come and pick him up. But Gerry, being Gerry, wouldn't allow her to drive him. Cheek, I call it,' she smiled to Mornay, 'especially after you'd taken the trouble to come and pick him up.'

'You were in hospital recently?' Brad took up when Claudia seemed to have momentarily lost her thread.

Mornay felt herself growing paler and paler and could hardly believe that this nightmare was happening when she saw Brad look over to the babe as if to gauge how old he was, then heard Claudia proudly tell him, 'Luke's four weeks old next Monday.' And as Mornay wanted to groan out loud that her sister was telling him *everything*, her limbs suddenly seemed to have seized up, causing her to feel powerless to move. Then Claudia went on to add yet *more*! 'It was over that young scamp's arrival that I wouldn't have been surprised if my sister never spoke to my chauvinistic husband ever again.'

'Oh?' queried Brad politely.

'I'm sure Brad isn't interested,' Mornay found vocal release to put in hastily and huskily.

'But of course I am, Mornay,' he replied gently, and Claudia needed no more encouragement than that to reveal all.

'According to Gerry, Mornay was in quite a state that, after they went for a celebratory drink to wet Luke's head, Gerry afterwards put a dent in her car when he missed his turning and ran her car into a brick wall.'

At that point Mornay murmured a quiet, 'Excuse me,' and went into the house to telephone for a taxi. There was nothing that Brad 'eye for an eye' Kendrick did not know now, and nothing she could do to stop him from using as he would the information which Claudia had so eagerly supplied.

Mornay made her call and went back out into the garden wondering what on earth Gerry had been thinking of to have told her sister any of it anyway. It did not take her long to find out about that, however. For, as if she was starved of adult company and conversation, Claudia was still giving forth about the wretched dent Gerry had put in her car when Mornay—avoiding looking at Brad—joined them.

'Gerry was really worried, Mornay,' her sister told her sincerely. 'I don't think he was going to tell me about it, but when I could see that something was on his mind and badgered away at him to tell me what it was—he just had to confess that he didn't think he was your second-best friend any more.'

'Dope!' Mornay murmured, and was grateful that Luke at that moment awakened and seemed bent on impressing the neighbourhood with the prowess of his lungs.

Fortunately, a short while after that, the taxi arrived. Courteously, bearing in mind that Luke was yelling his head off, Brad said goodbye to Claudia then, without a word to Mornay, went striding to retrieve his belongings from her car. Without a backward glance he then went to the taxi.

Quickly Mornay followed. 'Brad!' she urgently called his name. He turned and, waiting for her to state what she wanted, looked at her with grim hostility. 'You— you won't . . .' Her voice faltered. 'Please,' she rephrased what she had been going to say, 'please don't—d-do anything to . . .' Her voice faded when she saw the murderous glint in his eyes. Without a word of farewell, he turned and got into the taxi, and Mornay watched the taxi drive off with fear entering her heart, certain in her knowledge that Brad Kendrick was not the sort of man to sit back and do nothing.

Mornay began to be aware that she was not on her own when, despite the fact that Luke was refusing to be pacified, her sister came over to her, and as if she had been having the most tremendous battle in holding down her curiosity ever since they had arrived, yelled over the top of Luke's cries, 'Who—was *that*?'

Mornay sought for words, looked away from her, and replied, 'Here's Gerry.' She had a small breathing space when Gerry drove his car on to the drive, braked, and Emily, Alice, Florence and Prudence tumbled out, and came rushing over crying her name.

'That's enough!' Claudia laughed, not very authoritatively, it had to be said. 'Mornay doesn't want your ice-cream-sticky fingers all over her clothes.' She was shooing them inside for an all-round hand-washing session when, 'Hello, Mornay—how's things?' Gerry greeted her, bestowing a brotherly kiss on her cheek.

He looks worried, Mornay thought, and told him, 'Fine.' What with four young ladies all wanting individual attention, and young Luke making his presence known, all was bedlam, and there was little chance of more than bitty conversation.

By the time a bed had been made up for her, and the children were safely tucked up and all was quiet, however, Gerry had been acquainted with the fact that a man named Brad Kendrick had driven her to his home and, staying only a few minutes, had left by taxi. Mornay had not missed the worried look that had again come to Gerry's face, and even though she feared that there was a great deal of trouble ahead she doubted—had it been possible to have a private word with him—that she would have confirmed she thought he was right to look worried.

She knew she was wrong not to warn him, but if Claudia, seeing him worried about something, had ferreted out of him that he had dented her car, then she would soon get from him that Brad Kendrick had cause to, and might well, bring a case against him. And that, together with the realisation that a driving ban spelt doom to her security, would do nothing whatsoever to improve Claudia's state of depression.

So Mornay smiled and did her best to appear as though she was in the best of spirits—and she guessed she had succeeded in making believe that there was nothing at all wrong in her world, for the worried look left Gerry, and Claudia seemed far from depressed.

'You're feeling better now than when I rang this morning, aren't you, love?' Mornay asked her.

'Yes, thank goodness!' Claudia replied with a heartfelt sigh. 'Everything seemed to be on top of me earlier today,' she added, and apologised, 'I'm sorry about being such a pain when you rang. I felt terrible about it after I'd put the phone down——'

'It's understandable,' Gerry cut in, and Claudia sent him a loving look for his understanding.

'Did anybody ever tell you that you're the best husband any woman could ask for?' she teased him.

'I'm going to make some coffee before Mornay gets the impression that you're glad you married me,' Gerry grinned, getting to his feet.

'So,' said Claudia the minute he had gone, '*who* is he?'

'I thought you'd forgotten,' Mornay played for more time, having had plenty in which to try to think up something convincing to explain the total stranger whom Claudia had never even heard her mention.

'Is that likely?' Claudia queried, and added, 'I purposely didn't ask you about Brad Kendrick in front of Gerry in case you felt a bit—um—shy about telling about him in front of anyone.'

'Oh!' Mornay exclaimed, and realised at once the track her sister's mind had taken. She supposed then that, given that apart from Robert Naylor she had never brought any other man-friend to her sister's home, and given her reluctance to talk about Brad, her sister's conclusions were perhaps only natural ones. But as if it were manna from heaven, Mornay grabbed at the explanation Claudia had offered her. 'Brad's—er—a bit—er—special,' she confessed, and was not lying.

'I thought so!' Claudia replied.

'It didn't show in my face, did it?' Mornay asked in sudden panic.

'Of course not,' her sister assured her stoutly, but had Mornay panicking again when she asked, 'Where did you meet him—while you were away with the parents?'

'I...' Mornay said, and, knowing that she was on tremendously shaky ground here, 'I...' she said again, and ducked the question entirely by saying, 'I'm a bit... Do you mind if we talk about something else?'

Mornay hated herself when Claudia, her look fully comprehending, murmured gently, 'Poor love, you've been knocked for six, and don't know yet how Brad feels about you.'

Mornay went to bed that night and reckoned she'd got a very good idea of how Brad felt about her. Never would she forget that murderous glint that had been in his eyes before he had left in the taxi.

She spent a most dreadful night, when she would waken again and again to find Brad's face with that murderous glint in his eyes swimming in front of her. Curiously, though, at the self-same time, there was an ache like a void within her that Brad was not there in the room next to hers. She missed him, and wanted him near.

Unable to sleep as she was, she could have wept from the pain of knowing that she would never see him again. It was during her wakeful hours, though, that it came back to her how the newspaper had said that no one ever put one over on him without living to regret it.

She was awakened by the baby crying on Friday morning and remembered how she had hoped Brad would never find out that she, by virtue of not telling him that Gerry had been the one driving her car that night, had put one over on him. What, she began to panic, would Brad do?

Leaving her bed, Mornay hastily washed and dressed and went down the stairs, still feeling rock-bottom at the thought of never seeing Brad again, while at the same time she was inwardly a mass of agitation that the next piece of Royal Mail to drop through Claudia's letterbox would be a summons addressed to her brother-in-law.

How much or how little Claudia had told Gerry of their brief conversation about Brad last night, Mornay had no idea. But with Gerry wanting to get to a particular site by eight, and with the rest of the early-rising household a thriving multitude of activity, there was no time as the day got under way for any sort of private conversation with him.

She spent a busy morning giving the house a blitz while Claudia, with three daughters at school, in between keeping three-year-old Prudence amused and attending to the whims of baby Luke, tackled a mountain of ironing.

Mornay still had plenty of space in her thoughts for Brad, however, and he was much on her mind when Claudia broke through her thoughts, and queried, 'Penny for them, Mornay?'

'My thoughts are worth more than that,' Mornay returned lightly, but realised then that if she didn't want her sister to begin to conjecture about her, she had better buck her ideas up.

By three that afternoon, though, as Mornay walked with Claudia to collect the children from the village school, her head was again in turmoil. What was Brad going to do? Would the weeks she had spent in Scotland with him count for nothing? She had thought him a fair man, but she kept remembering his aversion to having one put over on him, and felt that she was going crazy wondering whether his fairness would stand the test of her having done just that.

Back at the house an hour later, her doubts and fears had grown worse instead of better, and Mornay knew then that she was going to have to take some action or go potty. 'Can I use your phone?' she asked Claudia while the courage to do what she must was fresh about her.

'Of course. Come on, you lot, we'll go out into the garden and see if we can find a shady spot for a picnic,' Claudia at once prepared to make herself and her family scarce.

'There's no need...' Mornay began.

'There's every need,' Claudia replied. The very fact that she hadn't asked with her usual sisterly familiarity whom she was going to ring told Mornay that she knew something was troubling her, and that she was going to ring Brad Kendrick 'You can't even think when they get going, much less make yourself heard.'

Five minutes later, Mornay, after at first shying away from making that call, had given herself a short lecture and had then proceeded to find out the office number of Kendrick Components. Taking a deep breath, she then dialled that number, and while she waited for her call to be answered she renewed her lecture which had gone along the lines of the fact that, with Brad's office likely to close in an hour or so, not to make that call would mean that she would have to sweat it out until Monday to make contact—if by then he had not—through the legal system—made contact first.

'Kendrick Components, good afternoon,' said a pleasant voice.

'Miss Boulter, please,' she requested, feeling fairly certain that she'd have been wasting her time in asking for Mr Kendrick direct.

'Helen Boulter,' said an efficient-sounding feminine voice.

'Ah, Miss Boulter,' Mornay said quickly, 'It's Mornay Haynes here—can I speak with Mr Kendrick?'

'I'm afraid he isn't available at the moment,' her call was instantly blocked. 'Can I take a message or can anyone else help you?'

Mornay calculated that this was perhaps normal office procedure for anyone unknown to the secretary trying to get through to speak to Brad, and she put a light laugh into her tone as, 'Oh—I should have said, this is a personal call—if you'll tell Brad that it's Mornay, I'm sure that——'

'I'm sorry, Miss Haynes,' Mornay found herself blocked again, 'but Mr Kendrick is abroad on holiday.'

Mornay came away from the telephone feeling utterly defeated. For a few moments then she got angry—it hadn't taken him long to pick up his passport and fly off, had it? As swiftly as her anger had come, though, it as swiftly died when she began to wonder—had he stopped by at his lawyer's on the way to the airport?

She spent the next hour having a picnic with her sister and her offspring and in trying to appear as though she felt loads better for having made her phone call. In actual fact she felt worse than ever, because suddenly she was jealously certain that, as well as stopping by at his lawyer's on the way to the airport, there was every probability that Brad had stopped by to pick up the recipient of the two dozen roses.

A short while later Gerry came home, and as his daughters made a fuss of him Claudia made him a cup of tea and asked him how he felt about taking the family *en masse* to the late-night-opening supermarket.

'En masse!' he jokingly shuddered, and asked, 'Is it essential?'

'The cupboard's bare,' Claudia informed him.

'Then supermarket it is,' he agreed cheerfully, and, indicating the cup of tea in his hand, 'Just give me a minute to recuperate,' he added, 'and I'll be there.'

'Do you mind if I don't come?' Mornay suddenly piped up, that word 'recuperate' suddenly stirring a memory to life.

'Chicken!' Gerry teased.

Fifteen long minutes were to elapse before Mornay waved her sister, brother-in-law and their five children off, and was able to sit down and quietly think through the idea which that word 'recuperate' had suddenly sparked off.

Hurriedly she went back over her phone call to Helen Boulter, in which Brad's secretary had told her that he was abroad on holiday. But, Mornay then wondered— was he? Hadn't she been in the same room with him when, prior to their going to Scotland, he had instructed his secretary, 'And Helen—leave it twenty-four hours before you announce to anyone interested that I'm recuperating abroad'?

But he hadn't been abroad, he'd been in Scotland, and his secretary had known that because it had been she who had arranged Brad's 'hideaway'—so where did that leave her now? Mornay wondered anxiously.

Quite clearly Helen Boulter was an efficient secretary who would obey her employer's instructions to the letter. Had she, Mornay had to ask herself, merely been obeying his instructions to tell anyone interested that he was abroad, and was Brad, in point of fact, actually still in England?

Three minutes later, Mornay knew that there might be a way of finding out. Her stomach was churning away inside her when, the telephone number of the bungalow in Kilcaber indelibly imprinted on her mind, she found the area code and proceeded to dial. She swallowed hard as she waited—and then discovered that she had no need to be nervous, for Brad wasn't there—at least, if he was, he wasn't answering the phone.

Replacing the receiver, she sighed, feeling quite fatigued with the emotion and trauma of it all. It seemed imperative that she contact Brad, but by then it was becoming hazy in her mind whether she wanted to contact him because her top priority was to prevent him from doing anything that would jeopardise her sister's security—or if she felt it so urgent to contact him because she was desperate for the sound of his voice.

Mornay knew Brad would not still be at the Belvedere when she looked up their telephone number. He hadn't even booked in for so much as last night, she knew that as, feeling compelled by she knew not what, she began to dial. All he'd done was to stay long enough to settle for the garaging of his car and then he'd been off, and headed straight back to London.

'The Belvedere Hotel.'

Quickly Mornay got herself together. 'Would you put me through to Mr Bradford Kendrick, please?' she requested—and got the shock of her life when the receptionist told her to hold the line a moment.

Mornay surfaced from her shock to realise that the receptionist would come back at any moment now and tell her that she was sorry but that Mr Bradford Kendrick was not registered.

But the receptionist did no such thing, and Mornay was left dumbstruck when she came on the line again and told her, 'You're through now.'

Mornay opened her mouth, and then closed it when no sound came. But no sound was coming from the other end either, and that alone forced her to try to get some sound out of her vocal cords. 'B-Brad?' she eventually managed to query, and very nearly collapsed when he replied,

'What kept you?'

'I—d-didn't know where you were,' she told him, stupidly, she rather thought, for his tone had been more toughly sarcastic than genuinely enquiring. But silence was all that came from the other end and, forced to go on, 'What—are you going to do?' she made herself ask.

'About what?' he asked, sounding terse and unbending.

'About Gerry,' she replied, and felt her nerves tensing as the silence from the other end stretched.

Then, clearly and quite distinctly, he arrogantly told her, 'You'd better come and find out.' Then the phone went dead.

CHAPTER NINE

TWENTY minutes after putting down the phone after her call to Brad at the Belvedere, Mornay was still trembling. Her first instinct had been to get to her car and to get over to the Belvedere as fast as she could. But life wasn't as simple as that. For one thing, she was not in her own home, but in Claudia's, and since her sister and her family were out and she didn't know if they had a house key she realised that she would have to wait for their return.

In any case, she realised an hour later, she didn't think she was ready to face Brad yet. She wanted to be calm when she saw him again, but she was far from being cool and collected. She looked down at the cotton shirt and trousers she had worn all day, and in the next moment she was haring up the stairs to take a quick shower and change into a smart linen two-piece. She then applied a small amount of make-up and pinned her blonde hair into a classic knot, and then she stood back to observe in the mirror that the cool female who stared back at her and who wore just a hint of sophistication bore no resemblance to the totally all-over-the-place person she was inside.

Mornay was human enough to be pleased with her appearance as she went downstairs to wait for Claudia and Gerry to return. She had taken the two-piece with her to Scotland, but had not worn it, so Brad had never seen her in it, nor, so far as she could remember, had she worn her hair this way while they had been together.

Not, she thought a moment later, that he'd give a fig what she looked like; he was more interested in her nerve in daring to lead him up the garden path over who had been at the wheel of her car that one particular night.

Agitatedly Mornay flicked a glance to her watch. Should she ring Brad and tell him that she couldn't leave the house until her sister and brother-in-law returned from shopping? On the grounds that he would think her an idiot, she decided against ringing him.

In all, though, she had to wait over two hours since she had made her call to Brad before she could obey his command that she 'come and find out'. She was at the window when she saw Gerry's car approaching, and she was out of the house, her car keys in her hand, by the time he had pulled up.

'I've got to go out,' she went to Claudia's open window to tell her.

Whatever Claudia felt like saying, one look at Mornay's solemn expression made her hold back. 'I'm sure it'll be all right, whatever it is, love,' she said quickly, and earned Mornay's gratitude for not prying.

Mornay was driving off down the road before the children had been released from their safety harnesses. The nearer she got to Reefingham, though, the faster her heart began to pound.

She was hoping with all she had as she pulled into the parking area of the Belvedere that she still looked as outwardly cool now as she had looked in the mirror in her bedroom at Penny Dale—because never had she felt in such a haywire state of agitated turmoil.

Leaving her car, she tried to keep her expression impassive as she went into the plush interior to the hotel and approached the reception desk. 'Could you tell Mr Kendrick I'm here?' she asked of the smart male on duty, and was just about to add her name when she discovered that that wasn't necessary.

'Miss Haynes?' the man enquired with a charming smile, and, when she murmured that she was, 'Mr Kendrick is expecting you. I'll get someone to show you up.'

In next to no time she, who had assumed that her interview with Brad would most likely take place in the hotel lounge, was in the lift being escorted upwards. Mornay had time only then in which to feel most relieved—since she had a fair idea that she was in for some of Brad's acid—that she was to be spared having that acid heaped on her in public. Then the lift was stopping, and before she was ready for it her escort had taken her to one of the doors in a long corridor, and with a pleasant smile departed.

With a shaking hand Mornay tapped on the door in front of her and, when a feeling of wanting to run away presented itself, she had to firmly remind herself that her purpose in being here was to ask Brad what he proposed to do about Gerry.

Then the door opened, and there, tall, dark-haired, dark-eyed and arrogant—and just as she remembered him—stood Brad. She saw his glance go from her face, flick over her slender linen-clad figure, then up to her smooth hairstyle and back to her face. He looks tired, she thought, and was not conscious of thinking anything for many minutes after that when, the first to speak, 'Did you walk it?' he enquired sarcastically as he stood back to allow her into his room.

She knew he was referring to the length of time in which it had taken her to get there. 'Claudia and ... I had to ... They went to the supermarket—I had to wait until they got back. I didn't know if they'd got——' She broke off, realising that she was babbling in her nervousness, and walked past him to discover that she had crossed the threshold, into not an ordinary hotel room, but a suite of rooms.

'Take a seat,' he invited laconically, as he closed the door, walked across the carpeted sitting-room of the suite and indicated one of the two settees drawn up before a fireplace.

'Thank you,' she murmured politely, and was glad to sink down into its padded depths. With her ankles neatly draped one over the other, her long legs at a slanting angle, Mornay endeavoured to look doubly cool to make up for her show of nervousness earlier. But, aware that the utmost tact was called for, she hardly knew where to begin. 'You—said to come over,' she reminded him for starters.

'Which—in due time—you did,' he replied gravely, which, as he availed himself of the settee opposite her, was of absolutely no help at all.

'You know why I'm here,' she told him.

'Remind me,' he suggested, quite infuriatingly, Mornay fumed, because he had a brain, more of one than most, and she doubted that he ever forgot a thing.

But she felt better to feel angry; it took the edge off her nervousness at any rate, as she coolly told him, 'I want to know what you're going to do about...' Her voice started to fade as her anger fled and nerves started to bite again, '...about G...my brother-in-law,' she made herself finish.

'Ah, yes, Gerry, the man who rang you when we were in Kilcaber,' he drawled.

'He rang to see if I could come back to give Claudia a hand,' Mornay explained.

'Which was after you had rung him to let him know where you were.'

'I had to ring him—don't you see that I had to?' she began earnestly. 'No one knew where I was—well, except Mr Probert—he's my boss,' she inserted, and saw then Brad had not forgotten that call from her flat to her boss, and went on, 'Well, he thought I was with my mother. Anyway,' Mornay rushed on, not seeming able to stop now she had started, 'it was important that Claudia didn't guess that I wasn't at my mother's, which she might have done if Robert Naylor had rung her——'

'Rung your mother?' Brad cut in, right there with her so far, Mornay was glad to see.

'Yes,' she nodded. 'Actually, had I known that Robert was and probably still is in Wales, I wouldn't——'

'You've not seen him since we got back yesterday?'

Mornay shook her head; in actual fact she could not remember giving Robert so much as a thought since she had returned. 'No,' she told Brad, and thought she saw an easing in the aggressive way he had been looking at her. She knew herself mistaken about that, though, for his aggressive look was there in full force as she resumed, 'If I'd rung Robert first instead of Gerry I'd have known——'

'You rang Naylor too from Kilcaber?' Brad sliced in to snarl.

'I...I...' Her nerves were back with a vengeance at the furious glint that came to his eyes. 'I—er—rang his firm—but he wasn't there for me to speak to——'

'What did you want to speak to him about?' Brad fired, and suddenly Mornay started to get just a bit fed up with his constant, questioning interruptions.

'Because he's my boyfriend, that's why!' she snapped, but when Brad glared more fiercely than ever, and indeed seemed as though he would leave his seat on the settee to more forcefully press some point home, she went rapidly on the defensive to tell him, 'I just wanted to prevent him from ringing my mother.'

'Why would he do that?' Brad gritted annoyingly, and Mornay had a feeling then that he was being obtuse on purpose. Though what any of this had to do with why she was there, she failed to see.

Though, because Brad was the piper and he was calling the tune, there was nothing for it but that she should reply to each and every one of his questions—no matter how annoying. 'Because,' she began stiffly, 'I could see, if Robert tried to contact me at home and I wasn't there, that—as Claudia would have done similarly—he'd either ring me at work, in which case Mr Probert would tell him I was staying with my mother, or he'd ring Claudia, who would tell him the same.'

'Which would see him ringing your mother and sub-sequently setting the fox among the hens when your mother told him you weren't there,' Brad took up, more than able, as she had known, to work it out for himself.

'Exactly,' she replied.

'Weren't you afraid Claudia would ring you in Solihull for a chat? From what I've seen I'd have said you and your sister are very close.'

'We are,' Mornay confirmed, and was a degree or two softened by his insight. 'But Claudia and my parents have—er—grown apart over the years, and I thought I was safe for a little while there. When Gerry knew where I was he told Claudia that I'd gone away with my parents on holiday—and that—er—stopped Claudia from trying to contact me in Solihull.'

'Now why, I wonder,' Brad suddenly changed tack, 'would a husband lie to his wife?'

'You know *why*!' Mornay exclaimed.

'No, I don't,' he denied. 'I'm not even sure I know why you've lied your blonde little head off from the first moment you and I came into contact—verbal contact, that is,' he added drily.

'I—that...' Mornay stopped and started again. 'Gerry couldn't tell Claudia the truth about that accident. Don't you see, it would have worried her silly?'

'Why?' he asked, as at some stage Mornay knew deep down that he would. 'He didn't hold back from telling her of the dent he put in your car when he "hit a brick wall". So where's the difference—given that I got carted off to hospital and that he was the coward, not you, for not stopping.'

'I'd have said that what you've just said is enough reason,' Mornay muttered coldly.

'Why?' he repeated. 'No one got killed, and since it seems your drinking spree stayed at the one drink level, he wasn't likely to get summonsed for driving with excess alcohol in his bloodstream.'

Stubbornly Mornay kept her lips sealed. He had more than enough to hang Gerry now—surely, much as she loved Brad, she couldn't be expected to tighten the noose.

But, when about ten seconds of her stubborn silence had ticked away, she was suddenly discovering that she had no need to tell, or not tell Brad anything, for he had it all worked out anyway.

'Of course!' he said, and she knew then that, whatever he had been thinking about since the last time she had seen him, it certainly was not Gerry, or he'd have worked it out before this. 'Your brother-in-law's been up before the magistrate on a driving charge before, hasn't he?' Mornay still stubbornly kept her lips sealed—much good did it do her. 'Quite obviously,' Brad went on, his dark eyes boring into hers, 'Overton has sufficient points against him to know that another driving misdemeanour would mean the certainty of having no driving licence at all!'

'He needs to be able to drive to get himself to work!' Mornay uncrossed her ankles and leaned forward to tell Brad urgently. Then she sat back in her chair and could have groaned that, in her urgency, she had just about confirmed all he had just guessed at. Which left her with nothing but to beg, and plead if need be, for him not to give that information to the police. 'Can't you see that for the sake of Claudia's peace of mind, her security, for her and her five children, it would be almost as much criminal to report Gerry?' she said quickly.

'Criminal?' Brad questioned toughly, and Mornay could see that, since he had been the victim, perhaps her powers of tact were less than they might have been.

'Can't you see that, with my sister's security at stake, I should never have ventured anywhere near the accident wing of Reefingham General that day after the accident?' Mornay tried a different but still crucial approach. 'C——'

'But you did,' Brad reminded her levelly.

'I hadn't intended to,' she got side-tracked to let slip. 'That is,' she went on to qualify, 'I'd hardly slept the night before, and when I heard on local radio that you were in hospital and had lost your memory, I felt dreadful.'

'So you should!' he grunted toughly.

'I'd wanted to stop when we hit you,' she hurriedly told him. 'I was sure Gerry was going to stop, but he...' Her voice faded as she realised that she so wanted Brad's good opinion of her that her tongue was running away with her again.

'But he refused,' Brad finished for her.

Having brought herself up short, Mornay declined to confirm that, and said quickly instead, 'Anyway, when because of everything that had happened I couldn't concentrate properly on work the next day, Mr Probert thought it was on account of my worrying over Claudia, and——'

'She was having problems?'

'Nothing too great,' Mornay replied. 'She had a soaring temperature which caused her to have to stay in hospital for a couple of days longer than she'd expected. Anyhow, when, because of you, my work began to suffer, Mr Probert, thinking it was Claudia I was so anxious about——'

'You were anxious about me?' Brad asked quietly.

'Of course I was!' Mornay exclaimed. 'Anybody would be! What do you think I am?' she charged, and, realising that she would rather not know, she went rapidly back to what she had been saying. 'So Mr Probert told me to take an hour off to go and see Claudia. First, though,' she slowed down to continue, 'although I knew quite well where the maternity wing of Reefingham General was—I found myself in the accident wing.'

'Your conscience had brought you there to see me,' Brad suggested, not unkindly, she thought, but though she had lied to him before, she discovered most oddly just then that she could lie to him no more!

'I didn't intend to come and see you,' she found herself confessing. 'I got my geography wrong and thought the side-ward you were in was Sister's office. I—er—got the shock of my life when I saw you there.'

'You knew me straight away, didn't you?' he questioned, and even if Mornay could have denied it she saw that there was little point. He'd remember from the way she had straight away started talking about the accident that she had recognised him—when it later became plain, by virtue of the ward sister's appearance, that no one had told her where he was.

'You looked directly at me,' she told him. 'Just before my car hit you, you looked straight at me—I . . . I knew that I'd never forget what you looked like,' she said shakily, but felt more shaky than ever when Brad, as if the initial nightmare she had gone through showed in her face and had stirred him to feel compassion, suddenly left the settee he was occupying, crossed the carpet in a couple of strides, and came to share part of the settee she was on.

Then, as if that wasn't enough to totally unnerve her, he looked deeply into her wide blue eyes and murmured softly, 'Poor Mornay, you've been to hell and back, haven't you?'

'I—er——' she choked, and just couldn't believe the gentleness which she suddenly thought she saw in his eyes. It must be, she realised, that, having been aggressive to start with, Brad had decided to use a softer tactic before he delivered a death-blow to her hopes of getting him not to prosecute Gerry. 'Er—did you recognise me straight away?' she asked, that being the only question to come into her head that had any sense to it since she had just mentioned that Brad had looked directly at her. 'You—er—said, at the hospital—that you'd not lost your memory at all,' she belatedly recalled.

'Neither I had,' he replied, his tone evening out as any genuine softening there might have been in him faded, and he adjusted his position to move a few inches away from her. 'Though of the accident I remember nothing. All I can remember is waking up in hospital and the nursing staff telling that I'd been the victim of a hit-and-run driver. Then, while I'm still trying to sort my head out, along comes a most beautiful red-carnation-carrying blonde.'

'Oh,' escaped Mornay on a little gasp. Then, fearing that he might have caught a glimpse of what it meant to her to hear that *he* thought her beautiful, she sought hurriedly for some sensible remark. Though the only thing to come to her was, 'Er—actually I bought the carnations for Claudia.'

'I realised that a few minutes ago,' he stated, his tone entirely unoffended. 'I thought about you a great deal after you'd gone.'

'You—did?' she questioned warily.

'And then some,' he confirmed quietly, and, as she warily eyed him still, Mornay began to receive the oddest notion that Brad was holding himself in check. Somehow, she began to get the strangest feeling Brad was a man with a lot on his mind, a lot which, although it involved her, had little to do with the accident.

'It's—er—natural, I suppose,' she replied to what he had said, while at the same time she could not help but wonder if being in love with him had given her an extra sensitivity to his thoughts and feelings—or were her senses playing her entirely false? 'I'd—as you thought—just put you in hospital; it would be only natural that you'd—er—give me some thought,' she added nervously.

'Which is exactly what I told myself,' he murmured. 'What would be more natural than that I should be angry with your lies about seeing the ambulance come for me? Wasn't it only natural that I should be furious—when I cannot tolerate being ill or incapacitated, and have a particularly strong dislike of being in hospital—that through you, hospital was where I ended up?' he asked, but went on, not waiting for her to answer, a hint of warmth entering his voice, 'But why then, furious and angry with you, should I find myself also intrigued by you?'

'In-intrigued?' Mornay questioned chokily.

'What else?' he questioned in return, and effectively stilled any wild beating in her heart when he itemised matter-of-factly, 'How could I not be intrigued when, having run me down and seemingly driven off without conscience, this beautiful woman who stands every chance of getting away with it then turns up at my bedside when there's a great chance that someone will start asking questions?'

'I was—a bit stupid, wasn't I?' she mumbled.

'Not stupid at all,' he denied. 'Just basically a caring person, as I realised very early on.'

'Oh,' she murmured, trying to quieten loud, clamouring bells of alarm that warned he must not see just how 'caring' she felt where he was concerned.

'Though I rather think that your second visit to me in hospital would not have been so voluntarily made,' Brad went on.

'You ordered me to come and see you!' she reminded him.

'And you turned up later than I thought you should,' he inserted.

'And you were horrible to me,' she said without thinking.

'How should I be...?'

'I'm sorry,' she swiftly apologised. 'You were hurting, and——'

'It wasn't just that,' he cut across what she was saying, and then astonished her completely by adding slowly, 'I thought you weren't coming. I thought that you'd re-alised I'd no intention of having you prosecuted over the accident. I——'

'You weren't going to prosecute!' Mornay gasped. 'But—but... You mean I went to Scotland with you for nothing! You...'

'Hardly for nothing!' Brad told her sharply.

'Well, I suppose not,' she had to agree, remembering how rocky and without colour he had been when he had come out of hospital. 'You needed someone to look after you, so why not the person whom you thought had put you in hospital?' fairness made her agree.

'My sentiments exactly,' he concurred. 'Though, to be fair in return, I'd been ill before my meeting with your car saw me hospitalised.'

'You'd been ill!' Mornay echoed, unable to hold down her concern. 'What was wrong with...?'

'Nothing to worry about,' Brad told her, sending her a smile, a warming smile, at the concern in her voice. 'I was halfway to recovering from a quite severe bout of flu when I suddenly woke up to find myself in hospital.'

'This was after the accident?' she asked, and when he nodded, 'But you were in Reefingham working,' she said, clearly remembering him saying that he had come to her home town the night before a meeting to have a look round the place. 'You shouldn't have been working...'

'I'm used to working,' Brad said softly, and for some reason she could not fathom he seemed encouraged by her anxiety over his health as he went on, 'I'd worked more or less on and off all the way through flu, so I suppose it wasn't so surprising that when I woke up in hospital where I was forced to rest, I was also forced to face the fact that I felt exhausted.'

'You could have had pneumonia!' Mornay cried in alarm as her imagination took off. 'The shock of the accident together with your flu, could have brought on pneumonia!'

'You did a splendid job of looking after me,' he said gently.

'Oh, Brad,' she cried, and wished then that she'd known more about his health, and that she'd done more for him—though, since he wasn't at all keen on fuss, she doubted he'd have let her do more than she had.

'You're sweet,' he said, and suddenly, as if he could not resist it, he sent her heart wildly racing by leaning forward and placing a gentle kiss on her mouth. Then he pulled back and, looking into her eyes, he quietly told her, 'Don't feel too badly about what happened, Mornay, for I have to confess that one or two good things came about from that accident.'

'What good could possibly come from you being knocked over?' she exclaimed, and entirely missed the fact that she had moved from her defensive position where her brother-in-law was concerned to being quietly indignant on behalf of the man she loved.

Silently Brad studied her ruffled expression, then a warm look came to his eyes. Then, 'Perhaps I needed a few days' enforced incarceration in hospital,' he said softly. 'I should never otherwise have taken time out to pause and wonder why I found it impossible to let up.'

'You're a workaholic?' Mornay questioned.

'Let's say that, with my father's shiftless attitude to work before me, I determined from a very early age that I was going to be different.'

It was the first time Brad had mentioned his father, and Mornay loved him more than ever that he was letting her take a glimpse into this personal side of his life. 'I shouldn't think anyone could call you shiftless,' she told him gently, knowing for sure that no one got to the top the way he had without working jolly hard.

'I'll let you run my fan club,' he teased, and she loved him for that too. In love with him, and loving this time of suddenly being in tune with him, she was in no way going to spoil it all by taking exception to anything he said.

'When did you last have a holiday?' she asked him as the question popped into her head.

'Apart from Scotland——'

'Which was convalescence,' she put in.

'Which was convalescence,' he grinned, 'I can't remember the last time I had a holiday.'

'So being made to rest in hospital was probably just about what you needed,' Mornay suggested.

'That's more or less what I realised when I woke up feeling shattered, but not knowing whether it was from the flu, overwork, or if it could all be put down to my being knocked unconscious. When the idea came to me that perhaps it might be an idea if I let up a little, I promptly dismissed any such idea—and went to sleep. I seem to have done a lot of that—sleeping—in those first days after the accident,' he commented.

'You said yourself that you felt exhausted,' Mornay reminded him.

'Which is most likely why I couldn't be bothered to tell anyone who I was. I rather enjoyed being anonymous,' he owned. 'Not that it lasted long.'

'The manager of this hotel soon let the cat out of the bag,' Mornay remembered.

'True,' Brad agreed, 'And I spent some time sleeping and then waking to find that the notion I was dismissing, about letting up a little, kept returning. By the time you'd come to visit me that first time I must seriously have been thinking in terms of taking a rest—or at least I must have been on the way to realising that the time seemed right for me to take a distanced view of my life.'

'You'd never had time before,' Mornay commented with sudden empathy.

'It was for certain just then that I wasn't going anywhere in a hurry,' Brad replied, 'so what better time than the present to accept that I needed some time out from work to take stock?'

'You made a conscious decision to review your life?'

'I think it was more that, feeling flattened, the decision was more or less made for me. I knew that my company could run smoothly without me for a month—so began thinking in terms of finding a hideaway.'

'You didn't want any attention from the Press,' Mornay put in, and he nodded.

'But where to go?' he murmured, and added, 'I wasn't feeling fit enough to drive any distance.'

'So you thought of me.'

'It seemed logical,' he answered. 'Though I have to admit that you gave me the idea when the natural, caring you came through, and you began to protest that I couldn't leave hospital because I needed someone to look after me. I soon began to think—who better than you? And I was sure that, under the circumstances of your wanting to keep quiet your part of my being below par, you wouldn't be inviting the nation's newshounds round for a Press conference.'

'I made it easy for you, didn't I?' Mornay stated, and started to feel very mixed up inside suddenly—on the one hand she felt a chump for being so naïvely open with him, yet on the other she knew that she would not have missed knowing him for anything.

But, 'Easy!' Brad exclaimed in denial. 'You're joking!'

'But—you came to my flat and...'

'The alternative, when I decided to leave hospital, was for me to return to London, where it was fairly certain that my instinct to put my nose to the grindstone and keep it there was bound to surface. I felt at the crossroads in my life, Mornay,' he warmed her heart by confiding. 'I had a thriving business, I'd worked hard and got where I wanted to be by my own efforts—there was nothing left to prove.'

Mornay was silent for a few seconds, but, warmed that he had confided what he so far had, she glanced away from him in fear that he might read in her eyes how she reacted inside to his every entrusted word. 'So,' she got herself a little together to start questioning, 'you signed yourself out of hospital and came to my flat, and began to take stock, and...'

'That,' Brad said, 'was the trouble. I didn't begin to take stock.'

She turned her head to hurriedly look at him, 'You—didn't?' she asked, and saw him move his head slowly from side to side.

'Before I knew where——' Abruptly he checked, and quickly looked away, and Mornay had the clearest impression that he had been about to say something totally different from what he did say when he resumed, 'Before I'd been in your flat more than a few hours you were getting tough and telling me that I couldn't stay there.'

'Me—getting tough!' Mornay exclaimed, and could have hugged him from the sheer joy of it when he blatantly lied,

'I was frightened to death of you.' He paused, arrested by the amused smile that came to her mouth, and then went on, 'Your idea of Scotland suited me fine.'

Mornay's amused smile quickly departed. Scotland would have suited him fine, wouldn't it? she thought jealously, as she instantly recalled how he had visited his 'mother' in Perth while they had been in Scotland. 'Because it then gave you the time you needed to review your life?' she enquired, her tone grown cool.

'Review—hell!' Brad replied, and, when she looked away from him he sent her heart stampeding along by placing a warm hand under her chin and turning her head round so that he could see into her face. Then, quite distinctly, as her heart drummed rapidly away inside, 'Don't blow hot and cold with me, not now, Mornay,' he asked of her urgently, and indeed, he seemed to be experiencing something of the same inner turmoil that she had been in when, 'I didn't even begin to take stock,' he told her in such a restrained kind of way that Mornay again had the feeling he was holding himself very much in check.

'You weren't feeling well enough,' she suggested, her cool tone suddenly gone.

'Physically, I'd started to improve minute by minute,' he hit that theory on the head. Then, to make her stare, 'But how could I begin to sort myself—my life out,' he went on, 'when I discovered—that I was a total wreck about you?'

She felt utterly amazed by what he had just said, and her eyes went saucer-wide in her face. She tried, as nerves began to attack, to turn her head away from him. But Brad still cupped her chin in a firm, warm hold, and she could not turn her head away. 'W-what—are you—um—saying?' she asked croakily.

'I'm saying, my dear, dear, Mornay,' he answered, to make the blood course round in her veins even faster, 'that when, without exception, I've always had the ability to view everything clearly, objectively, within hours of meeting you my clear perspective had vanished—clouded by emotions which I didn't begin to understand. While my objectivity was likewise distorted.'

'By—er—emotions?' she asked faintly, having been pummelled remorselessly by her own emotions since she had known Brad.

'That's what I said,' he confirmed, and, looking into her agitated eyes, he took his fingers away from her chin and caught hold of her trembling hand. 'Before I knew what had hit me, there I was in the grip of emotions which I have never experienced before.'

'What sort—of emotions?' she just had to ask.

Without her knowing it, she was gripping his hand tightly. 'Jealousy, for one,' he confessed.

'Jealousy?' she whispered.

'Furious jealousy,' he agreed, 'at the thought that you might have a live-in lover.'

'Live-in . . .' Her voice faded in astonishment at what he was saying.

'I was still in hospital,' Brad took over to elucidate. 'I barely knew you, yet when you started to argue the toss about me not coming to your flat, and I realised you might have a live-in lover, I was staggered by the energy in the jealousy I experienced—until you denied my charge.'

'Good heavens!' Mornay gasped.

'If you're shaken, think how I felt,' he murmured. 'In less than twenty-four hours I'd met you and told you to come and see me the next day. Then, when you didn't come at the time I'd decided you should come, I'd grown angry with myself that not seeing you had the power to irritate me. And, all before I knew it, I was roaringly jealous over you and discovered—when you'd gone— that I was wasting no time in coming to find you.'

Mornay swallowed hard; she wanted with all her heart to believe what she thought Brad was telling her but, because it was so unbelievable, she was afraid. 'You were over-tired, ill,' she found excuses to put forward for his emotional state.

'Which of course is exactly what I told myself when I got out of bed early in the morning after that one night I spent in your flat.'

'I didn't hear you.'

'You were dead to the world,' Brad told her, adding, 'I suspect you'd been awake most of the night on that most uncomfortable of couches. Anyhow, I stood looking down at you and, as the most staggering emotion took me, and my heart began to thunder, threatening to fracture my ribs, I knew then why I had checked in the telephone directory for your address, and had taken a taxi to come looking for you.'

Quite desperately then did Mornay want to ask him her own 'Why?', but the sudden fear in her that he might be turning the tables on her and leading her up his garden path as her punishment caused her to hold back.

'You...' she cleared a constriction in her throat '...you—hmm—felt better when you went back to bed. You were back in bed when I got up to come and take a look at you,' she remembered. 'You smiled,' she said, quite without thinking, and could have died from the inanity of her remark.

'You looked so lovely standing there with your blonde hair all anyhow,' he murmured, casting a sideways glance at the classic knot into which her hair was now confined. 'But,' he went on, 'by the time we saw each other again at the breakfast table I'd realised that, while this new emotional side that had awakened in me must be put down to my still being affected by the accident, and I must therefore counteract it by checking any feelings of—pleasantness I felt towards you, I could not deny that it didn't suit me at all to have you suggest, as you did, that I was well enough to go home.'

'Oh?' Mornay queried cagily.

And Brad smiled. 'I wanted time with you, Mornay,' he told her softly. 'You'd told me I knew nothing about you, and I realised that I wanted to know all there was to know about you. So much so,' he went on when, dumbstruck, she just stared at him, 'that on our journey to Scotland, when you were so solicitous about how I was standing up to the journey, I began to realise that I was being more "pleasant" to you than I'd intended, and that I was starting to feel totally vulnerable where you were concerned.'

'Vulnerable—you?' Mornay asked.

'It was all so new to me,' he explained, but it explained little to her, and she was afraid to ask for a fuller explanation. 'Then in no time we're laughing with each other, and I'm trying to remember that I don't want to be vulnerable. But I am, because again I experience jealousy over your boyfriend. And then, suddenly, for the first time in years, I'm relaxing, and starting to feel great.'

'I'm so glad,' Mornay said simply, sincerely, and saw that Brad seemed to take heart from her simple statement.

'So am I,' he said, and caught a gentle hold of her other hand. 'I've suffered in more ways than one since I've known you, dear Mornay,' he went on softly. 'Will you not end that suffering for me?'

'I...' she said, and faltered. His eyes were fixed firmly on hers and she had to take a steadying breath. 'I'm not sure—that I know what you're asking,' she told him huskily.

'Have you not reasoned, from what I've been telling you, how things are with me?' he asked her, his voice gone as emotional as hers. Dumbly Mornay looked at him, afraid to blink, afraid to say a word. Then, 'My love,' Brad said, and, raising her hands, he placed a gentle kiss on each in turn. 'I've seen tears in your eyes when I've hurt you, and been afraid to follow you for fear I might take you in my arms to comfort you. I've subsequently spent the worst night of my life wanting to come to you, but settled for bringing you in a cup of tea the next morning when I was up and about, but could hear no sounds of you astir.'

'That was the morning after you'd been all—er—brutish—when you'd reminded me of the accident,' Mornay said nervously.

'That's right,' he agreed, 'and I so badly wanted to make up for being such a swine, I kissed you,' he reminded her, 'and then knew hell when, having torn myself away from you, the next time I saw you you had changed from being the warm and vibrant woman I'd held in my arms to being cool, cold, and giving me the "I wouldn't care if I never saw you again" treatment.'

'It—er—bothered you?'

'It sure as hell did,' he replied without hesitation. 'I just couldn't fathom what had happened in between our sharing of ourselves in your bedroom and your giving me the cold shoulder the next time I saw you. So,' he said, 'I had to ask myself—why?'

'You—would,' Mornay murmured, and felt her heartbeats speed up again when Brad leaned forward and gently laid a kiss on her cheek.

'The only conclusion my question brought me, even though nothing too alarming had taken place in those moments of our mutual embracing, was that you must be regretting that anything at all had taken place. That,' he said, and paused, and then, his eyes watchful on hers, 'or, could it be, dare I hope, that you had heard me sending roses to a lady and—were jealous?'

'I——' Mornay said, and had been ready to deny that she had ever experienced a moment's jealousy where he was concerned. But she hesitated. Brad could be leading her up some most dreadful garden path but—had she learned nothing of him in those weeks in Scotland? Oh, Brad, she wanted to say, please help me. Please tell me in words what you're saying. She had flicked her glance away from him, but suddenly she looked back at him, and could see nothing but sincerity in the dark eyes that held hers—sincerity, and a look that said: trust me. She swallowed hard once more, then asked him, 'Did you really go and see your mother that day?'

'Yes, Mornay, I did,' he replied at once. 'The roses were for her, too. It was her birthday, and I hoped to brighten for her what, prior to my getting on my feet financially, had not been too sunny a life.'

'Oh, Brad,' Mornay said softly, and was rewarded by a warm smile.

'My mother doesn't have the best of health,' he went on, 'but even so, I'd not intended to be away from you for so long.'

'Hadn't you?'

He shook his head. 'Having that dent filled in your car took forever to dry, and then it had to be sprayed over.'

'Oh, Brad,' Mornay sighed again, and at the loving look he bestowed on her it wasn't a question of trusting him any more, for it seemed quite natural that she was able to tell him, with only the smallest shy hesitation, 'Then—I was jealous all that day, and since then, for nothing.'

For perhaps two ageless seconds Brad studied her with a stunned look in his eyes. Then, suddenly, the most wonderful smile she had ever witnessed spread across his features. Then, 'My darling!' he cried triumphantly, and before she had taken another breath he had hauled her into his arms, and she was held fast against his chest.

Moments turned into minutes as, with Brad's arms iron bands about her, he held her as though never intending to let her go. Then, as if, like Mornay, he could not believe what was happening was real, his hands went to her shoulders, and he moved her gently from him and, keeping his hands secure on her shoulders, looked long into her loving, beautiful blue eyes.

Then, 'My darling,' he breathed again, and suddenly she was in his arms once more, and more bliss was hers when he laid his lips gently over hers, and then pressed tiny kisses over her face. 'My dear love,' he whispered, and again his mouth claimed hers in a long and loving kiss.

'Oh, Brad,' Mornay murmured shakily, held firmly against his heart, when his mouth left hers.

'You're all right, Mornay?' he asked, looking down at her, and she loved him more for his concern.

'Fine—now,' she told him, and saw him smile.

'Has it been the same hell for you that it's been for me?' he asked.

'I—think so,' she answered shyly.

'From the start?' he wanted to know.

'I . . .' she began and, when she hesitated, she saw him frown. But even as his frown arrived, he scrutinised her face and she realised that he must have read her shyness there, for like magic his frown cleared.

'For a man who's spent his life paying attention to detail, I've just slipped up very badly, haven't I?' he queried, and, not needing an answer, 'Forgive me, sweet Mornay, but I've been in such a hell of a state since your phone call that it's no wonder to me that I forgot to tell you the most important thing of all.' Mornay's eyes were glued to his when, first bestowing a tender, almost reverent kiss to her mouth, 'My heart, my world,' he said throatily, 'I love you—with everything that's in me.'

'Oh, Brad!' Mornay cried trembly.

'And it's the same for you?' he wanted to know.

'Y-yes,' she told him shakily, and was hauled tightly up against his heart for many long seconds.

Then Brad was putting some daylight between their two bodies, but he still had his arms around her when, looking nowhere but at her, he wanted to know, 'When did it start, this love I don't deserve, but need so badly?'

'I'm not entirely sure,' she answered as truthfully and as honestly as it now seemed she could only do. 'I can remember feeling quite glad to know that you had a housekeeper rather than a live-in girlfriend, so I think jealousy must have been at the root.' Mornay just adored him when he grinned in delight at her confession. 'And I can remember being most definitely jealous of the lady you were sending roses to. I knew that day that I was in love with you.'

Again Brad drew her close to his heart, and delicious moments passed for Mornay where Brad saluted her with tiny kisses and told her of his love for her and how he'd been afraid of frightening her off, while at the same time he'd been trying most desperately to gauge what, if anything, she felt for him.

'Honestly?' she questioned, wide-eyed.

'Honestly,' he confirmed. 'I came back from Perth and took you in my arms. When you didn't immediately push me away, I kissed you because I'd missed you, and spent the next few days in a state of wanting to take you in my arms again, but being too anxious in my love for you to risk it.'

'But you did—take me in your arms again, I mean.'

'Don't think I've forgotten,' he smiled warmly, and went on, 'Never will I forget the fury that raged in me last Sunday when Overton rang, and you had the nerve to tell me that you'd dared to ring another of your men-friends.'

'I couldn't tell you that he was my brother-in-law,' Mornay told him softly. 'Though I thought at the time the reason for your fury was because you thought I'd given away your hideaway.'

'Hideaway, nothing,' Brad growled, mock ferociously. 'My jealousy had just gone over the top, and I was hearing nothing more, seeing nothing more than my crazed belief that you'd cheated me by ringing some man behind my back. Only when you began to respond to my kisses, to being in my arms, did a modicum of sanity start to stir. Then, my love,' he told her quietly, 'when I looked down into your shy face, full sanity returned, and I knew that I had to leave you while I still could.'

'You knew then that I—er—wouldn't have—er—opposed you?'

'Forgive me, my love,' he breathed, 'but, yes, I did. But I also had to think past that moment. What if we'd made love and, when that time of sharing of each other was gone, you maybe got round to thinking that I'd seduced you, or worse, that I'd blackmailed you into giving yourself? What if you ended up hating me? What could I, who wanted you to give yourself in love, do then?'

'Oh, Brad, I could never hate you,' she told him from her heart.

'Now you tell me!' he teased, and hugged her to him, and reminded her of the grim days that had followed when she had wanted to get back to Reefingham. 'You'd said, "You don't need me!",' he backtracked, 'and I knew then that I needed you more than I needed anything in my life. That for me there was no life without you.'

'Oh,' Mornay sighed, and Brad kissed her hair and, as if he quite liked her present hairstyle, but wanted his Mornay back, he gently removed every one of the confining hairpins.

'Do you mind?' he asked, as he ran his fingers through her long blonde tresses.

'Not a bit,' she smiled.

'Good,' he said in a satisfied kind of way, and then went on to tell her how the strained atmosphere that had grown between them had really started to get to him.

'Then one day you jumped in alarm, I thought, when I came near you, and——'

'You slammed out,' Mornay clearly remembered.

'I went for a walk to try and get my thoughts together,' he confessed. 'I knew you wanted to return to Reefingham, but I was afraid that if I allowed that, then I might never see you again once we had parted. I still hadn't sorted out in my head what your jumping like that might mean. Were you afraid of my touching you? Were you scared of your own feelings if I did touch you? It was something of a relief, sweetheart, to find that the anxious state you were in when I returned had nothing to do with me.'

'I'd rung Claudia and she'd sounded tearful and said that she couldn't cope with everything, with a new son who never seemed to stop crying.'

Gently, Brad placed his mouth over hers, and pulled back to murmur, 'What could a man do when faced with his love being unhappy about her sister?'

'I'm sorry I lied to you,' Mornay told him quietly.

And knew how exactly they were on each other's wavelength when he replied, 'By implying that the new son and heir was older than he is?' He smiled wryly as he went on, 'I knew, of course, by the time I'd been acquainted with the actual age of that young man, pretty much all there was to know.'

'I'm sorry,' Mornay murmured again.

'So you should be!' Brad told her mock severely. 'It was so obvious that you'd got the jitters about my going any further than Reefingham that day that I began to suspect you didn't have a sister.'

'Really?'

He nodded. 'Our old enemy, jealousy, began to make me fairly certain that there must be some man involved somewhere. Which of course made me doubly determined to accompany you to the very last yard of your journey. And,' he added softly, 'am I glad I did!'

'You are?'

'Now I am,' he smiled. 'At the time I felt—to put it mildly—slightly murderous.'

'You—er—looked it,' Mornay remembered.

'How else should I look?' he enquired. 'I'd just met your sister, and within minutes I knew exactly why you hadn't phoned her to tell her you were leaving Reefingham. Within minutes, while you were losing some of your colour, I was hearing all there was to hear, all that in the weeks we'd been together you hadn't learned to trust me enough to tell me yourself.'

'I—couldn't,' she had to confess. 'Claudia means a lot to me. I'd gone with you to Scotland hoping that by doing so I'd sort of settle the bill for my car's having knocked you down. But the newspaper, the local one that gave an account of the accident, described you as a man who didn't like to have one put over on him, and—well, to be truthful, I thought you might see what I'd done in that light. I was still fearful about what you proposed to do about Gerry when I drove here tonight,' she owned. 'Even when I saw you—when we began to talk—I still wasn't certain, for all you said you'd no intention of prosecuting, that you weren't leading me on while you prepared to exact full retribution.'

'Ye gods!' Brad erupted explosively, and Mornay was seeing a coolness in his eyes again when, his arms dropping from about her, 'Do you still think that way?' he demanded.

But Mornay was no longer afraid. 'I love you, and trust you,' she told him simply, and was straight away hauled back into his arms.

'I once referred to the fact that you didn't know where the hell you were at,' Brad murmured against her ear. 'But those words have returned again and again to describe what I've been like. When I left in that taxi yesterday and booked in here I went through the hell of knowing that I'd fallen in love with a marvellous woman, and spent a long, tortured night, with half of me feeling that you should have known I wasn't going to prosecute, and the other half going through the nightmare of wondering if you had any feelings for me at all—other than fear. The thought that you might fear me, my dear, was worse than a nightmare. All I could do,' he ended, 'was to sit tight and hope with all I had that you would come to me.'

'You knew I'd ring?'

'I didn't know anything of the kind. I just hoped that if you were missing me a tenth of the way I was missing you then you'd phone. I just hung on, praying that, as I felt compelled to stay near to you, you, on whatever pretext, would feel compelled to get in touch with me.'

'By the time I did make contact, I was too confused to know if I was ringing to ask you not to do anything that might harm Claudia's security, or,' Mornay had to confess, 'if it was because I was getting desperate to hear the sound of your voice.' Tenderly Brad leaned forward and kissed her, and Mornay sighed from the beauty of it when he pulled back and looked adoringly at her. Then, softly, 'You wouldn't have contacted me?' she asked.

'I would never have allowed you to go out of my life,' he replied most definitely. 'But while I've been in hell all today, and wanting to contact you, I have at the same time been furious with you for what you've done.'

'What I've done?'

'You could have gone away with just about any man,' he told her severely, and when she just had to burst out laughing at his biased reasoning, he grinned too, and told her, 'You see what you do to me? I've waited and waited all this long, endless day for you to ring, and then for you to come to me. Then, when I'm fully determined before you get here that I'm going to remain aloof with you, you, within minutes, just by virtue of being with me, send all my pre-planning up in smoke.'

'Serves you right,' Mornay laughed.

But she sobered rapidly when, leaning back from her, Brad studied her solemnly for a few seconds, and then quietly let fall, 'Are we going to have your four young nieces as bridesmaids?'

'B...' Mornay opened her mouth, and had to swallow as a wave of emotion took her. 'Are—we—g-getting married?' she asked him chokily.

'Are you saying no after all you've put me through?' Brad asked, his expression unsmiling.

'I—wouldn't dream of it,' Mornay answered lovingly, and saw his wonderful smile start to break through again.

'Come here,' he growled gruffly, and then their lips met.

COMING IN 1991 FROM
HARLEQUIN SUPERROMANCE:

THE·BYRNSIDE·INHERITANCE

Three abandoned orphans,
one missing heiress!

Dying millionaire Owen Byrnside receives an
anonymous letter informing him that twenty-six years
ago, his son, Christopher, fathered a daughter. The
infant was abandoned at a foundling home that
subsequently burned to the ground, destroying all
records. Three young women could be Owen's long-
lost granddaughter, and Owen is determined to track
down each of them! Read their stories in

#434 HIGH STAKES (available January 1991)
#438 DARK WATERS (available February 1991)
#442 BRIGHT SECRETS (available March 1991)

Three exciting stories of intrigue and romance by
veteran Superromance author Jane Silverwood.

You'll flip . . . your pages won't!
Read paperbacks *hands-free* with

Book Mate • I

The perfect "mate" for all your romance paperbacks

Traveling • Vacationing • At Work • In Bed • Studying • Cooking • Eating

Perfect size for all standard paperbacks, this wonderful invention makes reading a pure pleasure! Ingenious design holds paperback books OPEN and FLAT so even wind can't ruffle pages – leaves your hands free to do other things. Reinforced, wipe-clean vinyl-covered holder flexes to let you turn pages without undoing the strap . . . supports paperbacks so well, they have the strength of hardcovers!

Pages turn WITHOUT opening the strap

SEE-THROUGH STRAP

Reinforced back stays flat

Built in bookmark

BOOK MARK

BACK COVER HOLDING STRIP

10 x 7¼ opened
Snaps closed for easy carrying, too